ERIK McHATTON

INTRODUCTION BY CARSON WINTER

The story, all names, characters, and incidents portrayed in this production are fictitious. No identification with actual persons (living or deceased), places, buildings, and products is intended or should be inferred.

Cover art by Enoch Duncan
Cover design by TJ Price
Interior art by Angel McHatton
Formatting by M. Halstead

First edition 2025

Reading advisories available in back matter for those who would like them.

Table of contents

For Noel, because life began again the day you took my hand.

introduction

Stories, ultimately, bring us together—passed around the campfire, between generations, from thousands of miles away. These repeated sequences of events are a common language, brought to life with characters who are us-but-not-us, in realms that are ours-but-not-ours, told in the distinctive voice of a teller whose cadences we capture and hold onto like a life raft—often times until our deathbeds.

Erik and I first crossed paths via an internet conversation about Thomas Ligotti. Ligotti, if you don't know, is something close to the ultimate *horror writer's horror writer*—inescapably bleak, idiosyncratic, all glued together with some of the best style in the game. Those who are into Ligotti tend to be *really* into Ligotti. So, for Erik and me, our first meeting was fortuitous. We liked the same stories. How could we not become friends?

Soon though, we discovered that we were both struggling authors too. Erik and I had somehow internalized our hero worship of storytellers and decided that we wanted to walk the same parallel path. In retrospect, it was no surprise that our writing lives became inseparable from our friendship.

We both grew, finding our voices along the way. And now, years later, I see the fruits of these labors in Erik's debut collection of short fiction.

I've read many of these stories over the years, smiling as I saw my friend reveal new facets of himself alongside previously unseen dimensions of his endless talent. But now, collected in a single volume, I'm not sure these stories can exist in any better form than how they're presented here, arranged in this order, side by side.

For those who are new to the work of Erik McHatton, I believe an introduction is in order. Erik is a student of the genre. He's read widely, with a keen critical eye. He has built his foundation on the old masters, and then followed their stylistic genealogies to the modern era. He has practiced and practiced, read and read. And because of this, he has become something of an amalgam of the history of weird fiction—a nightmarish gestalt of those who came before him.

Thomas Ligotti (of course) informs his philosophical, oftentimes absurdist approach (see: "We Must Be Rabbits"—a personal favorite). Clark Ashton Smith's eloquent, dense prose and fantasticism are also a key influence, one that rears its head and roars loudest in the final story of this collection, "Demodorum." Lovecraft and his cadre of *Weird Tales* writers echo across Erik's work as well, in pastiche via "The Last Case of Dr. Jonah Wexley Abbott" and through a subtler, stranger cosmicism in "Where We Are, Where We Were, Where We Will Always Be."

But what does Erik McHatton write about exactly?

Family, depression, the call of the void, poverty, art. All of the above and so much more.

What's most exciting to me about discovering a new artist is that by reading them, you come to know them. The highest compliment I can give an author is that I see them through their writing. And in *Straw World and Other Echoes from the Void*, I see Erik on every single page.

But we're talking about stories here. And if you want to peek at the man behind the curtain, then look no further than "Knocks"; where the power of storytelling to escape and catalog our personal worlds is as present and potent as the persistent, terrorizing noises from outside the family's homestead. Within the confines of a post-apocalyptic yarn, you can see its author hidden beneath the covers, flashlight out, mouthing the words of Smith, Howard, Bloch, and Derleth at midnight. That's the Erik I see in this collection—the student who has dedicated himself to an esoteric tradition, and now stands beside those same names he so reveres. Another worthy voice in horror's bloodline.

With its titular story, *Straw World* beckons you into a shared history. It greets you with wicked snark and a knowing grin. It reaches out with an unfamiliar hand that has turned the same pages you have turned, albeit with gnarled joints and crooked claws. It invites you to meet the author, a person just like you. And if you're anything like me, I think you'll be pleased to meet him.

Carson Winter
Saint Paul, MN
February 14, 2025

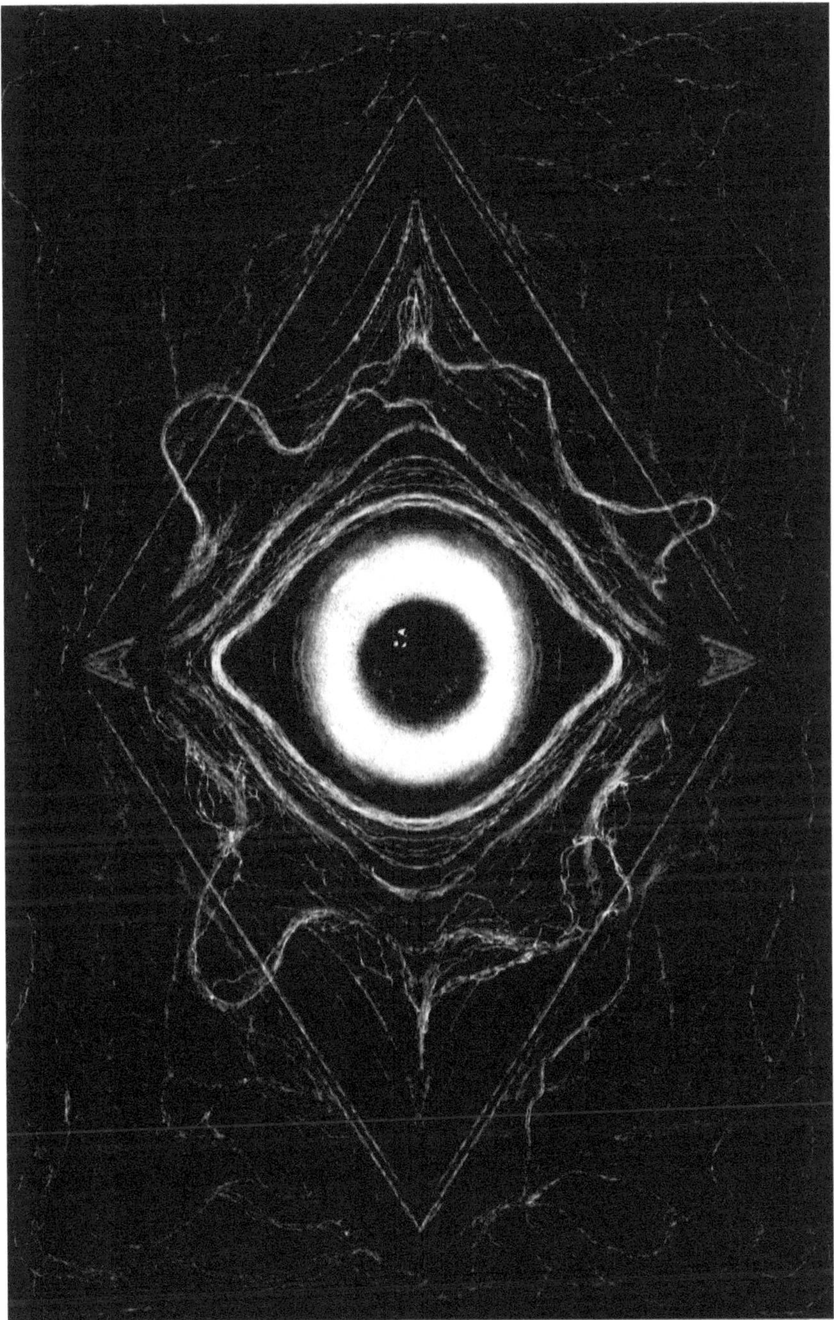

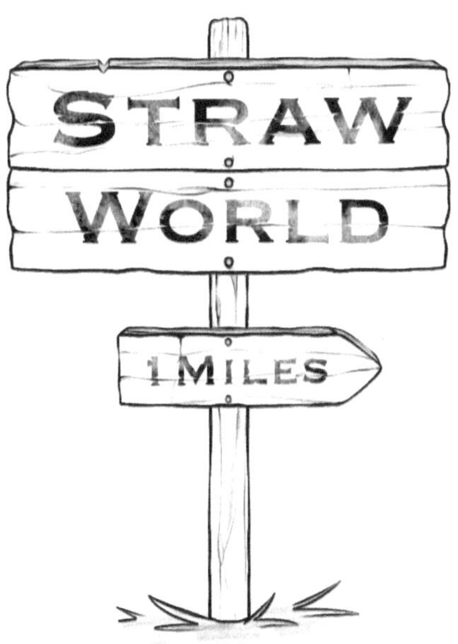
STRAW
WORLD
1MILES

STRAW WORLD

Hello there. Welcome to Straw World, the most unique art installation you'll ever see! Right this way, right this way. Y'know, you're the first visitor we've had today. We're so glad you decided to drop in. You won't regret it. This is going to be mind-blowing. You'll see. I don't mean to oversell it, but after this, you'll think of life in terms of before and after. Ha! I can see you're a bit skeptical; who wouldn't be hearing something like that, especially given the hyperbolic age in which we live, but I'm telling you, by the end, you'll be amazed. Absolutely gobsmacked. I promise. When I'm done showing you around this place, it will never leave you.

Straw World is the passion project of someone known only as The Artist. Pretentious sounding, I know. But what artist isn't at least a little pretentious? Tell me that. What they've—I say "they" because I've never actually met The Artist face to face, therefore I have no idea as to their specific personal attributes—done here is quite extraordinary but requires that we move through several different exhibits in order for you to be able to fully appreciate the experience. I understand this all may seem tedious, but if you give yourself over, the pieces will all fall into place in the end.

First, we go through the gate, the one there, at the end of the paddock. Do be sure to mind the rust. It'll be with you forever if you don't. I've made that mistake before.

Be sure to watch your step. The paddock is still in daily use. While Straw World does operate as a tourist attraction, there's not much money in it, sorry to say, so by day this is a dairy farm. See there, you almost stepped in a cow pie. You don't want that. The smell doesn't ever really go away, just stagnates. You know what I mean? It's one of those smells that you might not notice for hours or days at a time and then, BAM, it hits you when you least expect it. So, for the love of your sneakers, be careful.

Alright, we're coming up to the barn. The first stop. Now, you're going to think I'm crazy at first, that I'm far too enthusiastic for what appears to be a pedestrian display, but you just have to believe me. I know we don't know each other well, but for the duration I'm asking you to put such doubts aside. You have to learn how to appreciate Straw World. You have to ease in to get the full effect, like dipping into an extremely hot bath. I'll help you, hold your hand and ease you down, so to speak. I am your guide, after all. Okay? Now, if you look to your left, you'll see the first exhibit.

I know what it looks like. A row of scarecrow-like straw people dressed in old clothes, all shoveling hay. A bit hokey? Maybe. But look a bit closer. Look at the way The Artist has stuffed them, at the way the arms bulge, the legs ripple. Almost like real muscles, eternally taut, frozen mid-labor. Look at the form. Isn't that cool? The Artist is like one of those classical virtuosos who work in bronze or marble. A regular cow patty-dodging Michelangelo. You don't seem all that impressed. Maybe I'm not doing a good enough job expressing it. Let me try again.

It's not just the astounding musculature or the realistic way the clothes hang. These straw people—all the straw people in Straw World for that matter—have the quality of personality, of life. If you were to think very hard about them you can smell their sweat, hear the grunts as they hurl the hay over their shoulders. Try it. Really think about it. See? What did I tell you? Looking at these hay hurlers now I bet you can see them more clearly; see the people The Artist put inside them. And you probably didn't even look into their eyes. Those aren't just tortoiseshell buttons, my friend. They're just like our eyes, windows to the soul.

Let's move on to the second exhibit, the straw children playing out back of the barn. The hay forkers are only meant to prime you up! These kids, though, this is where things start to come together. Just look at their buttons, how they almost vibrate with life. This entire diorama, and all seventy of its kids, were given the most meticulous attention. The beauty of it still takes my breath away. Here, walk through them with me. Just imagine some kids who you knew or know, maybe kids you once played with. Maybe kids you have. What does their play sound like? Concentrate on the memory of that play. Conjure it. Put them on the swings, in front of the kickball, and see if you can't feel them living, just a bit. Look at their straw faces and see if they start to resemble the children you know. Hah, they do, don't they? I knew you could do it. Not everyone gets this place, but I knew you would.

See those houses over there; blue, red, and yellow? That's where we're going next. The Artist really hit their stride when they built these. We'll start where they started, with the blue house. The "happy home."

Come on in, wipe your feet and let's go into the dining room. That's where the action is here. See? A dining room table, a family reposed at supper. Mother so happy her family is fed, father heading up the table. The children, a son and daughter, perfectly positioned, backs politely straight up and down, hands clasped together in their laps. The Artist even added the family dog, lurking under the table for scraps. Look at the hope in his buttons! It's those tiny details that set Straw World apart. Seriously, sit down and take this in for a moment. Really let it inside you. Smell the air, I bet you can just sniff baking bread and broiled meat. Feel the hominess wash over you. Hard isn't it? The Artist found it difficult too, even though their work is impeccable. Something about it just wasn't right. Families aren't like this anymore. In Straw World it's important to match the exhibits with the personal experience of the viewer (as much as that's possible given the variety of people in the world), so a scene like this just doesn't connect. To most people this is a relic, held over from a time when we wanted this to be true. To some it's even insulting. It just doesn't fit.

The Artist began naming their exhibits with this one. They call it "The Lie."

On that note, let's move on to the red house.

The red house marks a shift in The Artist's goals for the artwork. There are more rooms to visit here as the family of this house is separated, scattered like cast bones. We'll begin upstairs. First door on the right.

Move aside, let me squeeze in. This is the daughter's room—a profile of a teenager in peril. From the posters, the black bedspread, the scratched-up photos stuck into the edges of the vanity mirror, one gets a sense of emotional neglect. Maybe you can relate in some way, or maybe you know someone. Picture the face of that relation twisted with the agony of being unseen, unheard, forgotten. Imagine their nights spent crying, screaming into pillows. How terrible it feels to have nothing and no one. Observe her carefully as she lies on the bed staring up at the ceiling, contemplating loneliness. Look at the pain in her buttons, the way the burlap stretches and shimmers around them, clearly marking the paths of drying tears. See how her muscles are almost all tight. How like a clenched fist she is.

Look closely at the nightstand. Do you see the straight razor? With just this implication one might conjure flashes of silver and red. Sprays upon the bed coverings. Slackness. One might place the razor into her hand and pull it across her throat in their mind's eye, killing the poor girl through mental puppetry, just as you've just done. And when you killed her, did she look like anyone you love? Horrible to think about, I know. But you wouldn't be here if you didn't yearn for darkness, would you?

The Artist calls this one "Unspoken."

At the end of the hall is the son's room. "Assailing" is its title.

We'll have to open the closet to find him, sitting inside, his knees huddled up to his chest. Head against his legs, face obscured, he holds his hands over his ears to drown out indistinct shouting from another room. You know the type, the kind of pleading you might hear coming from a neighboring apartment, praying for deliverance from heavy blows. This is the nature of the son's sorrow. He is terrified, rage-filled, ashamed of his inability to stand and protect. He wets himself with tears. And urine. Smell that now don't you? Ever know someone like this? Ever felt this helpless yourself? Who is this boy to you? Think of that person, let the feelings that brings up wash over you. Are you now fearful, angry, or ashamed? Or are you all three?

I told you this could be difficult.

C'mon, let's go to the parents' room.

Here, we'll just stand in the doorway. Okay, see the father at the end of the bed, the rippling tautness of his upraised arm, the flat palm about to strike. Look at the mother, cowered away from him on the floor, holding her arms defensively over her head. Can you hear his drunken shouting? Her whimpering? Have you ever known people like this? This man is that man. This woman that woman. This is where The Artist begins to ask for difficult things from Straw World's visitors. You *must* do as I ask for us to continue. It is no longer a suggestion or request. It becomes imperative from here on out that you put people you know into these exhibits, even if they don't exactly fit, and you must learn to carry out every implication in your mind. Strike the blow yourself. Let the sound of the slap reverberate inside you. Hurt as she hurts. Hear her cries for mercy. Allow him to continue on with none. Now turn away.

Allow yourself to feel the guilt of what you've just done.

This one's name is "Cascade."

Oh, and the family dog? Dead. Face blown off. Drunkenly shot for chewing on a prized slipper.

Which dog did you just think about?

This can be hard. I know. I'm sure you expected this to be a standard spookfest, but The Artist wanted this horror attraction to be much more visceral than any other. It must take a personal toll.

If you're ready, we'll move on to the yellow house.

The Artist built this house after growing weary of the blue and the red. You can ignore the sign on the door. The yellow sign, of course. I doubt you could make sense of it anyhow; I know I can't. I think it comes from some ancient language. The Artist loves old, dead languages. It speaks to their romantic side, I suspect. But romance has no place within the yellow house, so The Artist insists the sign is something else entirely. They say it gives the yellow house "horrible power." Maybe you've heard of such a thing, given your proclivity for horror stuff. Regardless, this is where The Artist's imagination really took off. Everything in Straw World outside of the yellow house is meant to be representative of the world that it mirrors. To those who reside within the straw out here, it probably feels close to normal. But inside this place, Straw World takes a truer, more terrible form.

I know if I were a straw person, I would much rather sling hay all day, swing on the swings, or live in the blue or even the red house, but never in the yellow. And most certainly not in the black. But we'll get to that later.

Before you come inside, however, you must know that the air in there is quite heavy and smells a bit foul. It reminds me of dead pumpkins rotting in the fields. You know that dead vegetable smell? Well, this place always has that quality. I suppose it's because of all the death it contains. Don't worry, though. It's not the kind of death you're used to. This part can be extremely uncomfortable. Even more than what you've already seen. If you're squeamish you might want to stop now and go back. I wouldn't think any less of you, honestly. Plenty of people don't have the stomach for darkness such as this. Some don't want to be so directly involved.

You're still with me? Fantastic! Okay try and ignore the smell and let's get inside.

Calling this one a house is a kind of misnomer, because, as you can see, it's just three large alcoves covered by heavy yellow curtains. You and I will go to each of these alcoves and perform a series of exercises designed to prepare you for the black, the big finale. Behind these curtains are experiments in horror, appalling straw sculptures completely unlike what you've already seen. The Artist has always had a taste for the macabre, but what they wrought here is otherworldly in its gruesomeness. Here, life and death are commingled in ways impossible in the natural world. You may think I'm overstating it, but in just a moment you'll see that I am not.

Before I pull this rope, remember, when this curtain opens, no matter what you see, you must do as I say. Everything hinges on your full participation. Anything less and we're just wasting our time. Alright? Good. Here we go.

This exhibit is called simply "The Mother." Look upon her prone body bent upward, as if offering herself to the heavens, her face contorted in something between agony and ecstasy, while her limbs, stretched in four extreme directions, are being ripped from her by black grasping hands emanating from the Void all around. Hear the sinews snap, the bones break as she's pulled to her limits. Her heart, still beating, *still* beating, exploded out onto her chest, sacrificed for those she cares for, her stomach distended, full and bulging at odd angles, forever holding its burdens within. Observe the way The Artist has captured the disparate torments of the mother figure. What a torturous thing it must be!

Look closer, carefully. Take your time.

You know what is next. You must now think of your mother and put her into this.

I do not know your mother, obviously, but whether you adore her or hate her (or something in between), this exhibit is designed to represent whatever she means to you. Perhaps it shows how desperately she sought to care for her young or perhaps it is meant to show remorse for the pain that she caused you. Hear your mother's cries now, as she pleads for absolution. Imagine the lagging beat of her dying heart as she gives everything for what she brought into the world. This is your mother. Repeat that to yourself and hold the image for a moment. She was ripped apart for you. Shredded. How does that make you feel? However it does, you must let it in.

I can see how upsetting this is for you.

When you're ready we'll move on to the next alcove. You might guess at what's inside.

"The Father."

Great, misshapen stones crush him as his head and limbs protrude out from beneath. Bloated, painted purple, as if about to burst, you can see his eyes bugged out, ready to explode. The stones, shaped like people, are piled atop one another in a great melded mass of responsibility. Look how his lips protrude, open slightly as if about to speak. Perhaps to cry for mercy or perhaps for more stones. His fingers are splayed out, grasping, looking for purchase on anything that might ease this burdensome fate. But to each side of him—hammer to the right, nails to the left—the instruments for building are forever out of reach.

This is your father. You saw his face, and I didn't even have to prompt you.

Did he abandon you in some way or did he hold you tight? Were there long days when his absence was keenly felt as the hours slid by? Did you ever feel as if you weighted him? Which of these stones is you? How heavy was your hindrance? If you took up his hammer would you place it in his hand or bash it against his head? Or would you instead lie beside him and accept some stones for yourself and be crushed by the same needs and expectations? Would you die slowly along with him as the stones pile high?

The next alcove is waiting. Take all the time you need.

This last one is the most personal of the three exhibits in the yellow house. I want to prepare you because this one is especially gruesome. It's called "The Child."

Behold.

Skinless, its inner straw exposed, "The Child" is stripped of identity. Those ribbons of flesh that have been torn away in tiny shreds from the bottoms of its feet all the way up its body—stretched from the top of its head and bowed out in the form of a cage around it—are the pieces of it taken off by those who were supposed to care. In their fumbling attempts to rear it, they instead peeled it every day. The yawning portal of its mouth moans with what has been done to it, calling out for its pieces to be put back. But even if one were to try, the strips of its skin would patch loosely together, overlapping, never properly healing. Look how it is splayed so like "The Mother" and "The Father," mimicking and beseeching its creators for providence. Look at the sorrow in its buttons, staring out of the bars of its skin-cage, knowing past wishing that it is forever trapped, never capable of flight. The air stings its exposed straw, cruelly.

Of course, this is you. You must put yourself inside the cage.

How were you failed? What are the causes of your soul's screaming? What cages you? Ask yourself these questions. Allow yourself to feel the unfairness of being born without consultation. Do this, truly, and you will be ready. Then, we will move on, through that door to the right over there, onward into the black.

C'mon. Don't be afraid. Get in here with me.

Good. Now shut the door.

Welcome to the last exhibit: "The Black." The Artist's greatest work. I need to tell you now, this one requires a substantial shift in your perceptions of reality. So far, we've occupied something akin to reality, at least the reality you're used to, but "The Black" is about *actual* reality, and, if you'll forgive the pun, you're going to have to keep an open mind. Understood? Good.

Now the first thing you'll notice is that you can't see. There is nothing around us, and, as such, we exist in a sea of possibility. If not for the absolute surety you have that gravity holds you to the ground, you might float about, tumbling in the air. But lack of physical illumination is not the problem, it is lack of elucidation on my part. Right now because of this ignorant blackness, it is only you, and me. If you need something to compare it to, think of how it must have been for you in the womb as you waited patiently for the world to open up to you like a burning eye. Think of this place as a vast, black Womb.

I apologize ahead of time for the subterfuge I'm about to reveal. Please believe me when I tell you the preceding theatrics were completely necessary. You see, this is not a story. I have not been speaking to some unknown character that you, the reader, have been half-occupying for the duration. If you were to go back and re-read the things I've said, you'll see that everything could have been addressed directly to you; was addressed to you. Now, considering these facts, I want you to try and re-contextualize the situation in which we find ourselves.

Are you still with me?

You might have made a few errors in your mental calculations, so I'd like to clear a few things up before we continue. While I am speaking to you from inside a written text, I am not a manifestation of the author's will. I am not the author speaking to you. I am a creature unto myself. An idea, born into the author's mind and pushed out into this "story." He dreamed me, and I taught him to create this place. Now, I've taught you.

My message to him, and to you, is simple. You and he and I exist in exactly the same way, we are all ideas carried around in someone's head. You probably have some idea of the author, even if this text is the only contact with them you've ever had. How strong of an idea, how clear the picture is, relies solely on the amount of information about them you've gathered. This is true for everything and everyone you've ever encountered. You see, there is something else you must understand before we can continue. It's a big one. It might be more than you can accept, but even if you don't believe what I'm about to say, just play along. Indulge me.

The universe is just data—an unending sea of information banging against itself, creating countless permutations of what could be: infinite impossibilities.

Allowing for this, what do you think you are? In case you still don't get it, I'll tell you.

We are merely possibilities, confluences, the endings of long series of events; eddies, rousted about by things of which we have no full conception. You are a drop in a boundless tide, unaware of what moons move you. Do you know how your great-great grandfather met your great-great grandmother? Even if you do, there are incalculable other variables involved in your existence. There is no way for you to ever truly know yourself, much less anyone you've ever known or loved. We all exist inside of the mind. Whether it is the imperfect portrait you have of yourself—the closest to the real "you" anyone could hope to know—or the mind-puppets of you kept by others, you are never more than an idea.

So, that means that everything you know, or have known, only exists to you inside this place, inside of the nothingness of your mindscape, where the two of us are conversing right now.

Here, you are a god.

But you are not omnipotent. You need guidance to create; inspiration, data. To imagine a chair you must have seen a chair. Go ahead, imagine one. Look! There it is, right on cue. Is it a familiar chair? Comfortable? The thing is, even if you try to defy me and create a new chair, one that you think doesn't look like any chair you've ever seen, you'll fail. You can only use external data to create amalgamations here. While the new chair might seem unique, it is still nothing more than an implication, made up of disparate parts of other chairs you've known.

Go on, sit down in your chair. Take a load off, for all that metaphorically matters, and think about how like the chair you are.

This all brings me to my point. As you may have already guessed, "The Artist," creator of Straw World, is really you, or at least you guided by me. The author and I created this place first, together, but its construction, like all "stories," is meant to force you to create it too, inside your mind. You see, if the universe is infinite, that means no matter where things exist, they are real, regardless of if the information is within or without. So, everything we've created on our journey through Straw World now exists inside your mind, as it does for the author and anyone else who makes it this far.

Now, back to the mind-puppet I mentioned. This is the crux of it, the purpose for the entire endeavor. If everyone you know is in here with you at all times, ever-changing with each new thing you learn about them, shifting perceptually with each passing day, then that means you've spent this time placing very real copies of them inside the "exhibits" I described to you. It is your mother, the one you keep, who is being ripped apart. It is your father crushed. It is you who will stand forever flayed inside your strip-skin cage, in here, in this pocket of creation you have wrought.

You just did it again. You see, your mind is as infinite a place as the universe, and everything you create in here is alive, not in any way you would understand or even be able to perceive it, but alive all the same. When you read any story where something horrible happens to the characters, you are doing it, you are the indifferent GOD that torments them for your own amusement.

You may dismiss all of this; you may think this is just the author trying to be clever. You might walk away and go tell someone about this story and how stupid you found it. "How pseudo-intellectual it all is," you may laugh. But we'll still be here. Even if you never read this again, we'll exist in the spaces between. Until your mind is gone, until you are erased, we will be. You'll think about this place from time to time, fleetingly, and you'll make another copy of it all over again. You'll see the razor slice. You'll hear the cracking of your mother's bones.

Maybe you enjoy this slice of truth. Perhaps, in your hidden places, you like the idea of knowing that the suffering you can create actually exists. Perhaps you are the worst kind of sadist. Perhaps I've given you a great gift.

There is no way for me to know from my vantage point who or what you are. After all, I'm just a construct myself, with limitations all my own.

But I do exist, and I'll continue to exist as long as this "story" is out there. I'll multiply, procreating with each new reader to make more of me, and together we'll do as we've done today, sculpt the stringy stuff of the universe into this place. And when the last person to ever have heard of or read this is gone, then I will be gone, because in an infinite universe the only law is impermanence. We all must eventually pass into the Void that waits on the other side of being.

So like straw; easily built, then blown away.

Wouldn't you agree?

Okay, now that my huffing and puffing is through, I'll leave you in whatever is left of the Straw World you live in. And no matter how long it is until we see each other again, remember, we're in here, all of us, the hay forkers, the playing children, the perfect family, the abusive cascade, your screaming mother, her rent limbs, your sputtering father, his bloated face about to burst, you, skinless, frozen in agonizing fear.

So, adios. Arrivederci. Au Revoir. Auf Wiedersehen. Goodbye.

See you again. Soon.

THE BLUE HOUSE

Knocks

As the knocking on the roof persisted through the night, Evie lay on her bed and stared at the ceiling. With the tip of her finger, she twirled a filament of cotton sticking out of her ear, and wondered once again about the nature of the thing above. Did it have feelings, motivations? Could it be reasoned with? Did it dream? Why did it want in the house so badly? She wondered if it could hear her thoughts about it. She wondered if she could command it psychically. She tried. *Get off the roof,* she thought at it. *Go away. Leave us alone!* Still, it carried on drumming the tin sheeting. Sighing, Evie turned over and looked out the window.

She was sure it must, at least, be aware of her. Lately, every time she went upstairs to sleep, it followed, leaving the others and clambering up the side of the house and onto the roof, settling just above her bed. The others didn't follow mother or father if they moved about the house. No, her parents' two creatures (if they were indeed assigned) stayed put on the porch, pounding at the front door both day and night. For some reason, Evie was special, if only to the thing that thought it was hers.

She pulled the cotton from her ears, dropping it into the bedside wastebasket before reaching into her nightstand to replace it. For those few moments the barrier was down, and the full cacophony of the knocking immediately overwhelming. She trembled as she pulled the new cotton ball apart and rolled it into two small plugs. She clenched her eyes shut, and stuffed the plugs in her ears. The snow crunch sound they made caused her to wince as she pressed them hard, much harder than was probably prudent, stopping only when it was safe, when she was sure of being back within the peaceful, muted world. Pulling her thick blanket over her body and head, she wrapped herself in muffling comfort and counted the dull, measured knocks like sheep. She drifted off, slowly, and dreamed of ewe-faced girl scouts and traveling salesmen with curled black horns.

After stringing together a few hours of under-nourishing sleep, Evie made her way downstairs. Her thing returned to its brethren on the porch, falling immediately back into rhythm with them. One, two, three; one, two, three. Sardonically, she waltzed into the kitchen to their cadence, breezing past her mother who sat face down at the table.

"Hello, Mother," she said without looking, reaching into the cupboard for her daily ration of crackers. Three today, two for tomorrow. After filling a dingy glass with sulfurous pond water from the tap, she seated herself across from her mother and stared at the balding crown of her head.

"I see you're finally away from the basement door," Evie muttered around a saltine. "How's the baby?" Her mother didn't move. If she'd given a response, Evie hadn't heard it. She didn't care anyway, just making conversation.

Finishing her crackers, she washed them down with the stagnant water while holding her nose. Not a single gag. "I think I might be getting used to the taste," she said, before getting up and gathering her father's meal. Three, no, two crackers for him. As she pulled his draught of pond filth from the sink, she stuffed his third portion into her mouth. He wouldn't notice. He'd want her to have it. Better that than to have Mother steal it again for the baby. The baby didn't eat, but Mother thought it did. How much food had she wasted by stuffing it under the basement door? It doesn't even have a mouth.

Leaving her mother in the kitchen to fend for herself (*and the baaaby*), Evie moved into the living room where her father lay bundled against the front door. He was awake and scratching in his notebook, his ear pressed firmly to the wood. He'd even managed to sit up on his own, a promising development. Both of her parents were uncharacteristically mobile this morning. After weeks of near inactivity, lying in their usual spots, messing themselves, Evie had feared they were both near the end. Truthfully, she hoped it more than feared it, but seeing them out of these destructive routines did make her somewhat glad. She smiled at her father as she dropped his crackers into his lap and sat the stinking glass down next to him. His eyes stayed fixed on the door; his scratching unabated.

"How are you today, Papa?" said Evie, crossing her legs as she sat close to him.

"Different today," he mumbled as Evie brushed dried bits of chewed crackers from his beard. While studying the knocks, he said little else. Always "different" he said, yet they always sounded the same to her. Whatever he heard in the knocking was beyond Evie. Whatever differentiation he sensed, she could not, as she could make no sense of the gibberish he scribbled in his notebook.

Her mother was the first of her parents to go, but her father followed shortly after, broken as much by his powerlessness as by the incessancy of the things outside. He had drowned in hopeful madness, called to the depths by drumming sirens playing songs of mispromised salvation. Maybe he believed that he could still save them, but Evie suspected that whatever now sat before her, swaddled in the trappings of her father, believed in nothing beyond the walls of its ensorcellment. To it, there was simply knocking, and listening, and scratch, scratch, scratching, broken up solely by the perfunctory interruptions of its basic survival. She was not its daughter, and it was not her Papa. It was nothing more than a living ghost, a being who answered purely to the call of otherworldly things, one who gargled on rations that could have been hers.

Wiping hot tears from her eyes, she snatched the crackers from his lap before rising and marching swiftly toward the den.

"Different today," he muttered after her.

Slamming the double doors of the den, Evie pressed her forehead against them, taking a deep breath before turning to face her late grandfather's library.

At some time in his life, her grandfather had acquired a taste for the fantastical and macabre. Aside from teaching, it was the only thing besides family he had any enthusiasm for. The result of this small obsession was a collection of tomes dedicated to the darkest imaginings of history's finest speculative minds. Books he'd shared with his granddaughter in his final days of life—books he left to her. Mother hated the idea, but Papa insisted she be given what was rightfully hers. Shelves from floor to ceiling containing rows upon rows of wondrous journeys wrapped around the room like an inviting hug, one that never failed to soothe her. For these last four weeks especially, since the succumbing of her parents, this sanctum offered serenity from the shattering of her world.

Of late, she found herself seized by a great wanderlust, compelled to spend her days within the room's embrace, traipsing from respite to respite. In the den, well away from the front door, through the cotton and oak, the barrier between her and the knocking was as thick as it could be. Only this gave her the ability to navigate those adventure-filled portals to passionate forgetfulness. Here she could concentrate wholly on crucial measures of dissolution as she melted from controlled into controller, taking within the stories a liberative command.

Throwing herself onto the antique divan, she reached for her latest escape that lay open on the end table, precisely where she left it. Placing another cracker in her mouth, she picked up the book, promptly found her place, and plunged.

It was the story of a terrible creature summoned by folly (as so many of them seemed to be) and featured a gruff protagonist racing to defeat the completely alien menace. Standard stuff, but the evocative prose enraptured, allowing Evie to hear the sounds and smell the odors of the horrible beast as it closed in on the hero; to feel the dread and ticking clock in her blood. She easily fell back into the story, and dashed from page to page with abandon, flying delighted through the dark and foreboding. The crushing reality beyond her head fell away and she was as zephyrous winds trailing just behind, witnessing the doom of another well-meaning man, a doom whose pace backward to meet the hero was determined by her will alone. And on this day, it hurtled.

She was gone for more than an hour before being jolted from her reverie by a faint rapping at the window of the den.

"No," said Evie as she lifted her head to see what she already knew was there. It was her thing, suctioned against the window, tapping at the glass with one of its gory protuberances.

"No, no, no, no, NOOO!" she cried as she threw her book down and marched across the room, grabbing at her stringy hair reflexively. She moved in tight circles before the window, casting hateful, panicked glances alternatingly between the floor and the intruder. "You can't be here. You always stay on the porch when I'm downstairs. Why should today be any different? Go back to the porch. Go back to your friends. This is my place. Only mine. You belong on the porch, so go back there. NOW! Go back, go back, go back. GO BACK!"

The thing carried on tapping, its amorphous body of mish-mashed and blended flesh undulating, its visible organs quivering with each thump. Evie turned her head and grimaced, reminded of how glad she was that they normally stayed well out of sight.

"You want me to go crazy like *them*, but I won't. You think because you came here, I'll give in. I suppose you think that soon I'll be some drooling mess, and then you can all come in and mop us up. That's what you want, right? That's why you've stayed outside, why you won't let me sleep. Well, I don't think so!" She returned to the divan to retrieve her discarded story. "I can read just fine, even with you here," she sneered, thumbing back to where she'd been before being interrupted. She read aloud, loudly.

"Brimley stood before the creature and watched as it coalesced into a single globular mass. Impossibly, it floated above the floor of the crypt. He marveled at the surface of its skin; so dark, so smooth. It appeared a perfect spheroid of nothingness hovering weirdly in the sepulcher's fetid air.

From inside this living chasm originated a humming, one that was proportionate to the sound he'd heard outside, the one carried by the wind. It circled into him, like water down a drain, emptying into his mind like waste. It bid him to come forward, to fall inside it, to adjoin with it.

Brimley reached for his ears in panic. Seizing them he—"

Her thing had stopped knocking. It merely sat there now, rippling oddly but not tapping, as if entranced. Evie crept across the room, goggling at the thing, attempting to tamp down the excitement that bubbled up inside her. Before she could get ahead of herself, however, the thing snapped out of whatever had taken hold of it and began going once again at the window, more intensely than before.

"I get it," said Evie as much to herself as to the thing. Reopening the book, she continued.

"...snatched vainly, as if to catch the trails of the humming before it could bore too deeply into his brain. It was of no use, and soon Brimley was limp from its possession. Jaws slack and drool dripping, he shuffled toward the portalous maw." Looking up, she saw that the thing had again stopped tapping, was again enraptured. Another promising development.

Evie and the thing finished Brimley's tragic tale that day, and made their way through many more before dusk came to claim the light and drive them up to bed.

That night, she noted that the thing's pounding on the roof lacked the fervor of previous evenings. It retained its autonomic character, to be sure, but all the verve had been drained out. Listless, she decided, was the right word. Perhaps it was daydreaming about the stories as she so often did, knocking out of sheer habit rather than at the behest of any conscious goal. Maybe she'd found yet another element the thing retained from its former human form. Knocking, then listening, now daydreaming. Might not reason be next, or at least close at hand? The day's events proved some understanding between them, and where understanding lay could not also compromise lie? She hoped this was the case.

She passed from her introspections into sleep and dreamed of the fields outside, those dead acres of farmland decaying around the house.

In her dream she hovered over the landscape like a witnessing specter and heard a great rustling coming from all sides. Louder and louder grew this rustling until one by one, droves of the things marched out of the woods with motions that had more in common with clumsy plopping than anything produced by footed creatures. They came, no doubt because they had finished with the more densely populated communities and had subsequently set their sights on places like the farm.

She saw the fields filled with thousands of the fluidic creatures pushing off and against one another, joined together in undulous dance. They bounced and wriggled, flopped and rolled, crowding closer and closer before merging into a single massive, rippling lake swirling with mottled flesh. The swirls then coalesced into moving pictures. Scenes projected from her mind's eye played out over the surface of their liquid flesh. There was Brimley tumbling down the gullet of Ohimbra, then came the flaying of the royal court of Hyphrovai. The crumbling of ancient Balaluud, the invasions of the Yephitarin hordes, all her favorite stories were shared across the protoplasmic expanse, conically echoing out from the casement of the den, onto which her creature still held firm.

She saw herself inside, her hand touching the window as she read, feverish eyes poring over offering after offering. She felt a wanting, titanous in its strength, to push through the glass and be bodily a part of those tales told through flesh. She would be transformed by their touch, melting and reforming, just like the baby (*the baaaaby*), like the gallant neighbor boy, like everyone she had seen overtaken by the creatures during her family's flight from the city. The possibility was no longer frightening, but welcoming. How could she ever have thought otherwise? Beyond the pane at her fingertips could lie the greatest adventure to which she'd ever been privy. She had only to accept their promise and it would be so. She was sure of it.

Finally, she saw the book fall from her hand, saw her white knuckles as she gripped at the base of the window. She saw it lifted and saw them flow through.

Awaking, Evie found that she had slept well and into the afternoon, carrying over from her dreams nothing but a vague sense of how important the previous day's revelation had been.

She buzzed through her start-of-day routine. In the kitchen, she gulped down her pond water without pinching her nose and grabbed a handful of crackers from the cupboard. She did all this while giving no more than a cursory glance to her mother, who still sat face down at the kitchen table, a putrid puddle having materialized on the floor beneath her overnight.

To her prone father she at least gave a grunt as she passed him on her way to the den. He could get his own food today, or her mother could get it for him since she was so interested in everyone's diets. Evie had more important things to do.

When she arrived, her thing was waiting. She smiled at its gory underparts as she plucked yesterday's last book from the divan. She then made her way over and sat before the window. It tapped delicately, almost politely. Pleased by its good behavior, she began.

After that, she spent nearly every waking moment reading to the beast and noted several patterns in its various reactions. Evie found that the thing enjoyed some stories more than others, and she became quite adept at picking just the right tales to tell. She fancied that a strange language formed between them, one that allowed her to glimpse into its alien mind and pull back the veil of its hidden desires. She even started to take her cotton out when reading. Her thing never let her down, never betrayed her, unlike her unresponsive parents, whom she found easy to abandon in favor of this new endeavor. Turnabout, after all, is fair play.

She began to sleep in the den, only stopping reading once the light died each day. She believed she had touched on its humanity, what remained of it at least, and in her nightly musings, when sifting through each day's events, she felt a growing pride, and even hope. Hope that she would succeed where her father had not; pride in being the one to save herself.

She barely ate from the boxes of crackers she'd taken from the kitchen, and expedited any bathroom needs by relegating them to the far corner of the room. There was no time for such unimportant things. Only time for forging ahead, and no amount of hunger or foul smell would deter her.

By the third week's end, she concluded that her thing was most fond of those stories in which the protagonists were overtaken and transformed in some manner, an unsurprising fact given the nature of the creatures' recent assault on mankind. It showed particularly intense interest when the hero thought of this transformation as a good thing, when they welcomed it. Its reaction to the thrilling conclusion of W.E. Hinson's "The Unused," in which an intrepid lad gladly merges with an incandescent lifeform, was enlightening. It scuttled and rippled for over an hour after the tale's completion.

After collecting this useful bit of information, Evie narrowed her selections even more and discovered that its favorite stories, the ones that caused it to fall from the window and roll about on the ground like an excited retriever, were the ones in which these transformations were not just welcome, but beneficial. Its response to Alphonse Dupont's "The Oblate Sphere" was positively apoplectic, orgasmic even. Evie watched it spread itself out in the dirt and dead grass, its surface bubbling and cresting in odd patterns, and could have sworn she saw the face of Dupont's farm boy melting into the god light in those patterns. Not long after this display, the answer came.

On the final night before the peace between them was well and truly struck, after considering every collected detail, she decided on one last yarn that would surely bridge the gap. She would read to it the tale of Usutrua, Queen Beneath the Waves, as chronicled in the inspiring work "Mother of the Fathomed," by the incomparable Wilhelm Schott. It was among her very favorites, and she was sure that it was the key.

The morning of her day of understanding Evie found herself overcome with an urgent, confusing sense of sentimentality and, owing to this, visited each of her family members in turn, even though by then they were all dead. She felt like her mother.

First came the baby (...but Charles, he's our *baaaaaby*!). Weak from malnutrition, she leaned hard on the basement's door frame and tried not to imagine him the way she'd last seen him, squirming and pooling at the bottom of his box before Papa sealed it up for everyone's safety. She tried not to hear again the frantic, pleading beats from inside as Papa had taken it down into the basement. She tried to forget how sorrowful mother's wails became when those pleas had stopped. Alas, there was no forgetting.

With her hand on the basement door she whispered quick and quiet; a promise, a prayer, and an apology. Sisters aren't supposed to hate. She would make it up to him.

Her mother, or what remained of her, was still slumped in her kitchen chair, purple face flat, flush against the table's dark wood. She was distended and split at the middle.

"I checked on the baby for you," said Evie, easing into the closest seat and grabbing her mother's limp hand. It squished a bit and she nearly dropped it. No, she had more strength than that. She knew that now. "He's just fine."

After offering up the same sentiments she had given to the baby

(Colin, *Colin!*), Evie stood and prepared herself for her last stop. She hesitated only a little at the thought.

She tried not to look into her father's eyes, staring at the ceiling—half-moons of darkened blood bowing beneath fogged irises—as she cradled his head in her lap. She stroked his brittle hair for several minutes, shaking off what caught and broke off between her fingers. She tried again and again to close his eyelids, but they eased themselves back open each time, as if to say, *This failure must be dealt with.*

"It will be Papa," she muttered. "It will be."

Later, sitting before her thing, criss-cross applesauce, book in her lap, she looked up at it with a wan smile spread across her face; eyes hazy. It had stretched itself enough to completely envelop the large window, spread so thin that it had become almost translucent, giving the world behind it the quality of gauzy gore. Organ clouds dotted the sky.

"I think I've finally figured it out," she said to it, patting the outside cover. "This story is the one, I just know it."

As she opened the book her thing shifted and bent outward, pushing its middle away from the window, tenting itself against the side of the house. Several tendrils of its non-Newtonian flesh extended outward from its center and pressed against the glass, smooshing together into a nebulous, hand-like shape. Evie knew exactly what to do.

She rose to her knees while plucking the cotton from her ears, and placed her hand directly opposite this extension.

Her thing palpitated with delight.

Awash in this delight, emboldened and encouraged by it, Evie moved her gaze away from the window and began to read.

Little Dirt Boy

A week after the funeral Agnes found one of his teeth. Her hand, stretched and sightlessly padding about the bottom of a stubborn drawer, fumbled across it while searching for a favored pair of sewing scissors. Her chest and stomach tightened as she pulled the small thing out and fresh tears came quick and hot as it rolled around her palm. It was the one he'd lost while trying to jump from the rope swing James made for him. *This was in his head once,* she thought dizzily while clutching it against her chest and falling to the floor. The rest of the afternoon was spent sobbing; the sewing, abandoned.

A week later, she got an idea. It crashed over her as she lay in bed, battling for another night the insomniatic curse that had plagued her since her son's death. Incensed, she dashed to her closet, found and took down the old Dutch packer trunk left to her by her mother. She tore through the pile of mouldered dresses and shoes before finally uncovering the family almanac tucked away at the bottom.

Adding to the book had been her sweet mother's favorite pastime, and in her waning years had become almost an obsession. Agnes herself had added nothing to the record since receiving it, a fact that bothered her only a little. She had no patience for silly things, and even less for most people. Nothing seemed sillier to her than keeping the useless history of no-count people living in a no-count place. Upon inheriting it, however, Agnes found she couldn't bear to throw it out. After finding the page she went excitedly searching for, she was certainly glad she hadn't.

What she looked for was an example of what her mother had referred to as "hilltop devilry," one of the arcane practices of the ancient hill people from which her family was descended. The ragtag tome was filled with all manner of primitive, hand-me-down recipes, spells and cures, along with esoteric rituals that were only sensible to the superstitious and the gullible, the weak and the desperate. While Agnes considered herself neither superstitious nor gullible, the death of her son had certainly left her weakened, driven to desperation by despair. Her grief threatened every moment to consume her as it continuously chewed at her mind. This was why she sought the hilltop magic that day, why she attempted to conjure a little dirt boy.

It was so very simple. She had but to wrap the tooth in a scrap of his clothing—after first covering it in a slew of herbs and oils—and then place the bundle inside a large ball of mud. Next, a burial in the back garden (which proved a harrowing experience being so close in approximation to the other) followed by precise chanting for well over an hour. The book's instructions called for only a quarter of that time, but Agnes wanted, needed, to be sure. If there was even the slightest chance a part of her dear boy's spirit could be returned to her, she vowed not to ruin it. Finishing the recital, she kneeled an hour longer before the newly wrought grave, and prayed to gods she claimed not to believe in with an intense, belying fervor.

That night, her sleep was easily won, but waiting for her, as always, was the dream, the only dream she seemed capable of dreaming since... since; a reliving of the awful incident that had stolen her child away.

They had walked deep into the woods behind the old barn, set once again on his never-ending quest for woodland oddments to marvel over. Be it a hollowed turtle shell, sun-bleached and beaming, or a tragic nest of broken eggs, he never failed to be astonished by the things he discovered in the loam and brush. Precocious and full of wonderment, he led her slowly on little fat legs, and she followed, soaking up as much of him as she could.

He had been so disappointed when they reached the ridge at the end of the old trail. He was never altogether happy at the conclusion of their explorations, but this time was especially frustrating as he had found nothing new to add to his collection. He sputtered about the clearing red-faced, and complained to the heavens with two tiny, balled fists. She stifled a laugh as he moved in furious circles, and tried to calm him, but he was tired and could not have his tiny tantrum tamped down.

Then he saw the bird.

Dried and maggoty, the body of a blackbird crowned a bed of moss at the base of a tree that hung precariously at the edge of the ridge. He picked it up before she could stop him and began squishing it between his hands, laughing. He'd never held a dead thing before, and didn't understand the difference between life and non-life. She was horrified at the slithering pupae squirming between his fingers, at the dead bird's eye falling over his knuckles. She cried out, and rushed toward him, knocking the putrid thing from his grasp. Startled, he stumbled. Stumbling, he fell over the lip of the ridge, and the only thing she managed to catch was one of his little red shoes as he tumbled, bounced and screamed through the dense, disfiguring branches to the unforgiving ground below.

Of recovering his body, and her frenzied flight into the village, there remains only ragged breaths, burning pain, and a cloud of overwhelming fear. Of her search in vain for help, only snippets, the swirling dreamfog carrying her swiftly from impression to impression with no real feeling of anything other than unrelenting guilt and misery. She always found herself in the same place in the end, however, dumped unceremoniously into a graveside seat in the family cemetery, staring at its newest hole intent on swallowing another of her loved ones. They'd dug it out between James's grave and her mother's, in the plot originally meant for her. *I killed him and gave him my grave*, she thought, pulling dully at her hair.

In the dream, as in reality, she was held tightly as she strained to reach the lowering coffin—held as she wailed, as she bargained, as she fainted. This is where the dream usually ended, with Agnes shooting up in her bed, lathered and panting. But not this night. On this night, she spurned the well-meaning graspings of her friends and neighbors and fell headlong into the hole after her child. She plummeted for what seemed like eternity before crashing down atop his earth-covered casket. Recovering, she threw fistfuls of dirt over her shoulder, slinging it in all directions, before finally exposing the lid and prying it open with raw fingers.

He was there, sticky with sap and blood, his dead eyes looking up at her accusingly, arms akimbo, splayed out like a ghoulish marionette. Now, she remembered. He appeared just as he had when she'd found him at the bottom of the ravine, and just as then she gathered him up and cradled him, weeping and apologizing. Placing him on one shoulder, she attempted to climb out of the pit, crying out to those above for help. Answering these cries, in lieu of assistance, came a rain of detritus as those above began to fill in the hole, and she slowly suffocated as she held her dead son and cried.

Her heart hammering, she awoke. Mistaking the pounding in her ears for a banging at the front door, she rushed to open it and there, on the doorstep, sitting exactly as he always had, legs tucked beneath it, was a little dirt boy.

She squatted to survey it. She prodded, gently, testing its solidity. Her finger came back mud-streaked and damp, much to her surprise. Doubts allayed, she rocked back on her bottom and folded her own legs beneath her in order to consider the thing properly.

Much more than superficially it resembled her son. This resemblance shone like the sun, and she found the need to look away several times to avoid a rising sorrow. Its muddy head was round like his, its face rightly lumpy in the nose places, the eye places, the lip places, the ears. Vegetative sprouting at the top suggested his ever-mussy hair, and its reedy appendages were draped inquisitively across its branchy lap in his manner of storytime readiness. Its trunk was rounded, insinuating an overly indulged appetite for sweets, and sticking straight out of its lump-mouth was an oily tooth, no doubt the one from which the golemic creature had spawned.

Satisfied, she scooped it up, ignoring her mud-stained clothes, and joyfully brought it inside.

The next several days flew by in a delirious haze. Agnes felt nearly whole again in the company of the little dirt boy, and in no time at all she settled into a routine that almost perfectly mirrored the one she had enjoyed with her son before his death. Aside from a few snags relating to its lack of appetite and animation, and the extra cleaning now required due to its pervasive filthiness, her life soon returned to an unsteady tranquility. If not for the tremulous feeling of wrongness dancing just outside the borders of her thoughts, she could have sworn that things were back to normal.

When she told it stories before they retired to bed each night, she imagined a slight smile crossed its irregular features. On those occasions when she took it walking in the woods, carrying it in a makeshift sling across her back, she was quite sure of the small yips and trills that it made when she pointed out wondrous things tangled in the flora. When preparing its favorite foods for their dinners (meals only she ate), she could just hear a growling coming from deep within its bulbous belly. In response to the announcement that there would be no more baths to worry about, she distinctly heard a small whooping from behind her while she caught up on the extra laundry at the creek. It spoke to her in its own way, and she was keenly receptive, as only a mother can be.

Unsure of how much of her son's memory the thing retained, she filled its days with tales of their recently lost family.

One afternoon they visited the rope swing and laughed as she told it of her hysteria at the profuse bleeding that followed its accident there. She reminded it of its father's kind words and manner as he managed the situation with his soft, calming hand. She then wistfully recounted several other delightful accounts of James's good humor, his kind heart, and of his generous wealth of spirit. After being reminded herself of how dear their James had been, she decided to walk it up the road to the abandoned wheat mill to show it where its father was working when he met his end not two years prior, and just like the day after James's funeral, she threw rocks at the sagging vanes, whooping and hollering with the dirt boy all the while.

She told it of her mother, and how wonderful it had been to have her live with them following James's accident. She made it berry tarts and baked apples, her mother's specialties, and even read to it from the family almanac in deference to her memory. She dressed it in clothes her mother had made for it, and sat with it in her mother's rocker while singing songs her mother loved, and which she claimed were as old as the hills themselves. She told it much about the good year they enjoyed together before that wretched illness came and devoured her mother's body and mind. She didn't speak to it of those last few months, of course; no reason to burden it with the memory of the gaunt, shrieking creature her mother became.

She dwelt not on sorrows, preferring laughter and revelry to morose recollection. In those days she came to love the dirt boy almost as much as her living son, and its company balmed the fierce aching that had previously threatened to overtake and drive her into the ground.

She enjoyed almost a month of this new life before the pastor came to call.

His coming was heralded, as ever, by the warbling whistle he was so fond of employing when making his rounds. She knew that a man of the cloth would never approve of hilltop devilry, and that the busybodies in the village just loved to gossip about such things, so as he breached her front gate and made his way down the walk, Agnes stowed the little dirt boy inside the packer trunk, right atop her mother's old things. She had just managed to cover with a sheet the tainted kitchen chair wherein the dirt boy usually sat, when the pastor's friendly knocking came fluttering at the door.

"Agnes dear, it's Pastor Willoughby callin'. I came to see how you're doin' darlin'. No one in the village has heard from you since the funeral. Ethel and the girls in the choir are simply beside themselves with worry. Oh do please let me in, if only to let me rest a while before I head back to town. It's powerful hot out here, beneath the mighty sun of God," he said in a singsong voice before chuckling at his pun.

She considered not answering. She was never one of his congregants, but he had presided over her funerals for free, and had been comforting when she had needed it the most. Reluctantly, she opened the door and afforded the pastor a broad smile.

"Pastor, how good of you to stop by. Come in, please, and sit with me in the kitchen. I'll put on some tea."

"Why thank you my dear, it would be a pleasure," huffed Willoughby as he squeezed his bulk through the cabin's small door and waddled after Agnes into the kitchen. As she busied herself with the tea, he plopped down into the unsheeted seat at the table and began dabbing at his brow with an embroidered handkerchief produced from his breast pocket. By the time the kettle crowed he had regained much of his composure, and his breathing had become notably less labored.

Accepting a steaming cup from her, Willoughby blew across its top before taking a careful sip. Scrunching his nose, he gave a loud "Woo!" into the air as Agnes took the sheeted seat across from him for herself. The moistness beneath seeped through and she hoped the pastor couldn't hear the soft squishing sound being made by her anxious shifting.

"My dear you always did make a fantastic cup of tea. Those old women in the village just don't know anythin' about the careful removal of bitterants," he said through a doughy smile filled with large, gleaming teeth, "but you darlin,' you know what you're about."

He tipped the cup in her direction before taking another sip and giving another dramatic "woo." Grunting, he stretched his legs before him and sighed. Sniffing at the air, he settled his gaze on Agnes as if waiting for a reply to a question he hadn't asked. Several moments went by, and his small eyes never wavered. Agnes squirmed.

"I've been doing quite well, you know. Quite well. I understand why the village might worry, what with James, and mother...and with my boy, but I'm managing quite well, quite well indeed. You needn't be concerned," she finally blurted, as she took a wobbling drink from her cup.

"Darlin,' I had little doubt, but you know how those girls get when they circle up for gossip, how annoying they can be once there's a buzzin' in their bonnets. So I told them I'd come by and see you, not just to put their minds at ease, but to save you from having to host the lot of them before the week was out. They don't think a woman can get by without a man to see to things, it's just how they are. No matter that I told them what a tough little girl you used to be, or about the tough woman you are now, they wouldn't have it unless I agreed to check," said Willoughby, finishing off his tea and putting away his handkerchief.

"Well, you tell 'em they have nothin' to worry about," said Agnes, subconsciously mimicking the pastor's drawl, "tell 'em I'm doin' juuuuuuuust fine."

Sniggering, Willoughby leaned forward and took Agnes's tight fists in a damp grip. He shook them up and down exuberantly.

"I will. I'll tell 'em I seen you with my own eyes and that your house was spotless as could be. I'll tell 'em that the front lawn was perfectly manicured, and that you made me some tea better than any pot they ever brewed. That'll stick right in their craws, I bet!" He chortled, then paused, his face becoming serious as he afforded her with another prolonged look. Without hesitating, Agnes cut right through it.

"What?" she said, somewhat harsher than she meant to.

"I wonder if you would want to walk up to your old family cemetery with me right quick? I'd like to pay my respects to them that's up there, to your momma and James...and to your boy too, if you'd like," he said solemnly.

Agnes took a moment, pretending to consider the offer. She didn't want anyone from the village anywhere near where her child had been buried, and after the nightmare she suffered before the coming of the little dirt boy, she didn't much care for the thought of going up there herself. Just thinking about it made her chest hurt.

"Thank you Pastor, but I don't think I'd like that. I do appreciate the kind offer though, and the next time I'm able to get up there I'll be sure to bring them your respects."

"I understand," he said, standing slowly with a groan. Restoring the affable grin he'd worn into the house, Willoughby clapped her on the shoulder before making his way back to the front door. Agnes trailed behind so as not to show the soiled wetness at her back, seepage from the covering sheet. When reaching the front step he turned to her, his deep concern barely hidden.

"You take care of yourself, you hear, and if you need anythin' don't you be afraid to come ask," he said, sniffing the air again before turning and heading down the cobblestone path. Without looking back he waved his hand theatrically over his head, saying finally, "You might want to check your attic dear, smells like something mighta' crawled in there and died."

As Agnes watched him disappear, whistling down the dirt road heading back into the village, she tugged at the grimy back of her sundress and had a sniff herself, only then smelling the smell she hadn't smelled at all before he'd come and smelled it for her; the musky scent of rot.

The stench bedeviled her every moment after the pastor's visit. She and the dirt boy searched the house for days, top to bottom, side to side, and could find no source whatsoever. The attic and root cellar held a number of desiccated things; rats, insects, small birds and such, but this was common in country homes. None of those corpses appeared new enough, or large enough, to give off the wretched smell from which there was now no escape.

Eventually, nonplussed and frustrated, she settled on the idea of airing out the house and filling it with bouquets of fresh-picked wildflowers in order to combat the stink. Unfortunately, there was no place on her land more suited for picking perennials than the open fields of the back acre, the ones set right against the hill on which the family cemetery was located. Regardless of this fact, she planned a picnic there for her and her dirt boy, vowing to not so much as look up to that detestable hill during what was sure to be a delightful outing.

As she left the reeking, unshuttered house the next morning, the limp boy slung carefully over her back, Agnes smiled into the dawnlight and swung her stuffed picnic basket at her side. A while later, they crested the southern slope that led to the field, and she stopped for a moment to consult with the dirt boy about just which spot they should spend their day upon. When satisfied with its answer, she made her way to it and spread out a checked blanket, emptying the basket before propping the dirt boy carefully against it.

She'd brought a smorgasbord of treats for them (her) to enjoy. A bottle of his favorite cider found secreted away in the root cellar was to be paired with a quarter wheel of cheese whose smell she was now slightly dubious of. Dried dates and currants and a loaf of day-old bread rounded out the bounty along with the pièce de resistance, a marvelous summer sausage made earlier in the year for just such an occasion. While nodding at a job well done, she looked to the dirt boy for its approval of her offerings. Its head was crooked to the side, but the queer smile it sometimes seemed to give was evident on its knobby face. This pleased her, and she ate and talked and laughed with it for several hours under the bright, unclouded sky.

Later, while filling her empty basket with wildflowers, she caught herself glancing up the hill despite vigorous promises not to. With every surreptitious peek came nightmare flashes that stole her breath and left her weak. Glimpses of a midnight flight through the fields and away from the hill. Fleeting feelings of being overburdened with madness while covered in sweat and soil. She severely bent or outright broke several stems in her contracting hands as she tried to calm herself and focus. It had indeed been a bad idea to come here, and she decided to leave and make do with what flowers she'd managed to not destroy.

Hastily, she returned to the blanket where she'd left the dirt boy to nap and violently shooed away a blackbird she found picking at its head. Gathering it up along with their things, she gave a final involuntary look to the hill, to its spiked crown of broken fencing, and shivered before making her way down the winding trail back home.

Getting back, she found the smell in the cabin to be markedly subdued. Delighted, she set the dirt boy in his kitchen chair and began vasing and placing the flowers about the house at precise intervals before moving on to the reshuttering process. When reaching the window nearest the front door she spied head busybody Ethel Stone ambling up the road toward her house carrying a covered pie. As she was no doubt intent on vacuous meddling, Agnes slammed the shutters, barred the door and dashed to the kitchen in order to block the final aperture. In her haste, she tripped and crashed headlong into the dirt boy, bowling it over and spilling it onto the floor.

Crying out, she picked it up and apologized profusely, stroking its brittle vegetable hair and kissing it as she moved to close the kitchen shutters. There was Ethel, pie dropped and stupidly gawking across the yard, still behind the fence. Placing the dirt boy quickly out of sight, Agnes attempted a casual wave which Ethel returned with an aghast, over the shoulder gaze as she hurriedly turned and headed back in the direction of the village.

She was discovered.

Her insides knotted as she had a vision of a rowdy, torch-bearing mob descending on her cabin, intent on righteous witch burning. She imagined Pastor Willoughby's fat hands wrapped around his holy book, bellowing in pious fury while fixing her with a rage-filled glare. She knew it was a silly thought, and she hated herself for it, but something inside her knew that the way she'd been carrying on was wrong, knew she should be punished for the blasphemy her life had become. She'd been attributing this feeling to her mother's superstitious parenting, to the indoctrination she'd endured during childhood and never fully been rid of. But looking at the dirt boy now, slumped over on the counter, she couldn't deny a deep and soulful shame.

By the time she was lying next to the dirt boy that night, she was feeling much better. She'd spent the evening stoking fires of resentment for those in the village. After casting off her brief, ignominious sentiment, she wondered how it was that they dared to make her feel it in the first place. The nerve of them galled her.

"So what?" she said aloud, staring up at the ceiling. "So what if they know about you. It's my business what I do in my own home anyway. I'm not even part of the village, technically, a fact that they've never been too shy to remind me of. It shouldn't matter to them what goes on here. Bunch of busybodies is all they are, showing false concern whenever there's trouble, never really helping. They just want something to talk about in that church of theirs every Sunday, something to make them feel superior, to distract them from their awful, no-count lives. I don't need them. I've never needed them, and I certainly haven't needed them these last few years.

"When your father died, and they brought him to me, I sent them away and cleaned him up myself. I'd have made the box he went in too if they hadn't done it first. I'd have dragged him up to that damned cemetery and single-handedly put him in the ground just to be spared their prayers and moronic condolences. Mother talked me out of it. She talked to me about 'community' and the 'brotherhood of man.' Pah! She trusted them too much, I told her so, and they proved me right.

"None of them, save the pastor and Doc Sutter, came to call when your grandmother got sick. They weren't here at the end. They didn't clean her, didn't watch her so that I could sleep. No, they just sent messages with their bland food, no doubt to placate their own guilt. But I managed well enough until there was nothing left of her to manage at all and *then* they came with more platitudes and prayers, bearing a fresh pine box. It was all I could do to keep from spitting on them.

"I should never have run to them when you had your accident. Now they think I've invited them in. Now they think they have a right to be involved. Let them come, then, and I'll tell them all, even Pastor Willoughby, to leave me in peace, and to never bother us again."

She turned on her side and looked at the thing to affirm her rantings. The dirt boy gave only a dull, vacant stare.

"You never hold up your side of the conversation," she said, laughing softly to herself as she pulled it close and drifted off into troubled sleep.

The next day, of course, they came. A delegation comprised of several men from the village marched up the road, headed up by the pastor, Ethel Stone and old Doc Sutter. To a one their faces were ugly with concern. She saw them long before they breached her gate and she prepared for their arrival accordingly. By the time they were on the front walk she had closed and latched all the windows and barred the front door. *Damn them and their false faces*, she thought as she sat down in the kitchen, clutching the little dirt boy so hard that it oozed.

There was a firm knocking at the door. No fluttering for Pastor Willoughby this day.

"Agnes dear," he said, trying and failing to keep his tone light, "please do let us in. Ethel swears she saw something terrible up here yesterday, something that can't possibly be true, and we just want to put her mind at ease. I know this is an awful imposition, but if you could let us inside we can have all this cleared up in a jiff."

"No, I don't think I will Pastor. I...*appreciate* your concern, but I have no desire to ease Ethel's meddlesome mind, and I don't feel I owe any of you any explanation for what I do in my own home. Now, if you please, I'd see you all off my porch and off my property. Go back to your village and pray for me if you wish, it's what you do best anyway," said Agnes, loud enough for them to hear.

The pastor's next words were more firm, less friendly.

"Now, dear, I'm afraid I'm going to have to insist. Doc Sutter is here with us and he's concerned as well, for your health you understand. He just wants to check in and see how you are. Ethel's got him all a tizzy with her imaginings."

"I seen what I seen!" Ethel screeched, and Agnes was overcome with an urge to choke the life from her. Fire ran through her veins.

"GO AWAY," bellowed Agnes, "GET OFF MY LAND YOU USELESS BUSYBODIES. WHAT HAPPENS HERE IS MY BUSINESS AND I'LL HAVE NO MORE OF YOUR GOD-DAMNED MEDDLING IN IT."

She heard the pastor exclaim "Oh dear" and then, after a brief moment of hurried whispering, there came a tremendous pounding against her door as the men outside sought to batter it down. Agnes began screaming obscenities and barely coherent curses, insisting they had no right, but they did not heed her. Within moments the door splintered and the conclave came pouring into her home. They tromped determinedly through the house before finally streaming into the kitchen where they all stopped abruptly, gasping nearly in unison in horror at the sight of her. Ethel vomited, then fainted away.

"Fine, have a look if you want you bastards," she cried, holding the dirt boy before her, peeling it away from her defiled breast, "it's just a little dirt boy, a bit of hilltop devilry I conjured up to help me get by. I'm not hurting anyone, you see? So now that you've seen it, now that you've had your fill of gossip, pick that witch up off my floor and get out of my DAMNED HOUSE!"

Shocked beyond speech they advanced and she recoiled from their encroaching, well-meaning grips, gnashing her teeth while attempting to shield the thing she now held behind her.

Then she was back within the nightmare, grasped and held firm while they pried what was left of her son from her arms. She screamed until hoarse as they carried her down the road toward the village, straining so hard she nearly broke her arms in the effort to free herself. Her mind unraveled as she watched two of the men leave her cabin, along with Pastor Willoughby, for they bore with them a carefully swaddled body. Consciousness was driven from her by the thought of where they were going with it, and what they meant to do.

They meant to travel the winding path and cross the wildflower field. They would climb to the top of that cursed and dream-fogged hill where all her loved ones lay. They would seek the hole that in her maddening grief had been exhumed, that darkened pit wherein they would replace the last of her worldly joy. They would bury it again, and she would be damned by their best intentions.

We Must Be Rabbits

Bumble wakes and finds Beeswax out of his cage again; asleep on the ground, his ears around his neck. Father may not be patient a second time. Bumble thumps, grunts, and hisses until Beeswax stirs, and sits up. Blinking, Beeswax grinds his fists into his eyes and looks across to Bumble blearily.

"Whaa…," he starts to say, but Bumble growls, cutting him off. Sounds, not words, are for rabbits.

Beeswax gets the message, shutting his mouth and yanking his ears up over his head before loping back into his cage, pulling the door closed behind him. He circles, and lies down, casting an anxious glance toward Bumble, who purrs his approval.

The commotion has roused Bramble, and Bill. They stretch and scratch themselves like they're supposed to, before drinking from their water dispensers. Their behavior is expertly executed, practiced to perfection. They have grown into fine rabbits. Each morning they do B Room prouder than the day before. Bumble purrs at them as well, and they purr in return.

A mostly successful waking. Father should be pleased.

The speaker buzzes, letting them know it's okay to leave their cages, and Beeswax is the first to do so. He awkwardly makes his way across the room to the toy area, doing his best to hop properly. He's only been in B Room a few days, so it's okay that he's awkward. Bumble isn't worried. Father never punishes those who are trying. He's very fair that way.

After a bit of play, their morning ruffage tumbles down the food tubes and out onto the floor. Bramble and Bill have no problems managing, of course, but Beeswax, being new, is still getting the hang of eating like a proper rabbit. No hands, no fingers, only teeth, that is how rabbits eat. As Bramble and Bill dive head first into their piles of kale, lettuce, mint, and alfalfa, Bumble helps Beeswax by going slowly, showing him how to pick through the leaves with his nose; to chew carefully, and furiously, just as real rabbits do. Being very new, it takes Beeswax more than a few tries to get it right, but by the time their carrot pieces are dispensed, Bumble is quite pleased with the progress he and Beeswax have made.

Their carrots are scarcely gone when the doors to their running wheels are opened, announcing the start of morning exercise. Beeswax has some trouble, but gets on mostly without Bumble's help. After a few failed attempts, he gets his wheel moving, and soon masters the gait of a running rabbit, his wheel going faster than even Bramble's, who Father has called the fastest among them.

The morning is going great, thinks Bumble.

The speaker crackles. Father's voice bounces off the walls. "Good morning B Room. The sun is shining and there are rainbows in the sky. What a wonderful day to be a rabbit! Please tidy your area and return to your cages. I will be with you shortly."

Tidying up takes little time, and soon they are in their cages, eyes forward, in their best rabbit postures, just how Father likes it. Bumble checks on Beeswax one last time. Beeswax is shaking—he's not quite used to Father yet—and his greasepaint has smeared from sweating. Father will have to reapply his whiskers for sure. That's okay, though. Father enjoys putting on their faces. Beeswax glances at Bumble, and Bumble risks a quick smile to reassure him.

The door buzzes. Father is here.

He tumbles into the room, a cloud of joviality; belly jostling, smile wide, yellow-white beard whispering against his chest.

"Hello my precious little bunnies. It is so nice to see you on such a fine day." Father spreads out his blanket, and with some effort manages to get himself seated on top of it. He pulls the paddle, paint tubes, towels, and bandages from the red, fuzzy bag slung over his shoulder. Bumble wishes he could tell Beeswax not to stare at the paddle. Father gives them all the signal that it's okay to come out of their cages, which they do, forming a semi-circle several feet away from him.

Once settled, Father continues. "First things first, I think we should start with commendations today! Doesn't that sound swell? I know we normally do lessons first, but things happened this morning that got me so worked up, I just have to talk about them right away!" Father picks up a tube of black greasepaint and uses it to beckon Beeswax over to him. "Beeswax, come here please. You're all sweaty from that positively magnificent display of running you performed this morning. Your face is all out of sorts. I'll fix you right up."

Beeswax makes his way over. He settles in front of Father, rolls onto his back and places his head in Father's lap. Father pats him, and begins rubbing the greasepaint off with the towel.

"Okay then, without further ado, the first commendation today goes to...Bumble, for being such a fantastic mentor to dear Beeswax here. A good teacher is an invaluable resource, and Bumble has really stepped up in this regard.

"Bumble and Beeswax. Such a clever pairing. Bramble, Bill, you two should take note of Bumble's unselfishness. For his efforts, Bumble will receive *two* gold stars on the board, instead of one. Isn't that wonderful?"

Father stares right at Bramble and Bill, who momentarily squirm before jumping into the air and clicking their heels together, performing simultaneous celebratory binkies. Father's smile never waivers, but does broaden as they leap. Bumble, for his part, never takes his eyes off Beeswax, who remains ever so still as his smeared whiskers are removed.

After Beeswax's face is clean, Father moves on.

"Now, the second commendation today goes to...little Beeswax here, of course." He looks down into Beeswax's eyes and lowers his voice, talking only to the young rabbit. "You've done so well in such a short time. I'm so proud of you. Before long you might prove yourself to be the best bunny B Room has ever begotten. I truly believe that." Father boops Beeswax's nose with his forefinger, and reaches for the greasepaint.

Without lifting his gaze from his lap, Father delicately applies Beeswax's new whiskers. When finished, he sends Beeswax over to his cage, and folds his hands across his lap, an indication that commendations are over, and it is time for the lesson of the day.

"Alright my rabbits, it's time for today's lesson, and while I know it's one that some of you have heard before, for Beeswax, it will be all new. So please, bear with me.

"Today I want to talk about the importance of conformity, which is the most important thing a rabbit represents to the wide world. You see, in their ecosystems, rabbits have no grand purpose. They are mostly insignificant in relation to other, greater things. Rabbits do not overreach. They do not pontificate, proselytize, or promote. They simply *are*. They jump, and run, and play. They sleep, and wake. They live. They die. And they do all of these things in service of very little, but do it in such elegant quietude; noble in their simplicity.

"To a fox a rabbit means exercise, and food. To a dandelion it means death and rebirth. These are simple, naturalistic, and warm meanings, important in a small, simple sense, but largely overlooked and forgotten by the world. This is tragic, but little tragedies happen every moment of every day, and why focus on that when one can instead choose to see the benefit, the beauty of it. Rabbits fill their role and they do it in a way that should be aspired to. You all are very lucky to be becoming like these gracious creatures, for there are so many other, worse things you could become.

"This is why I am teaching you to be rabbits. For one day, it will be your turn to go upstairs and meet a greater Thing. *The* Thing, the one that looks over us all. And when you do, it is so important that you know how to fill a rabbit's place, because there is no room for other, grander things before that Thing. As far as it's concerned, it is the only *thing* that matters. In the moment you are placed before it, to be anything other than a rabbit will mean certain doom. And I don't want that for any of you. I want you all to live as long, and as happily as a rabbit can. It breaks my heart every time one of you is lost.

"So, remember what I've said. Use it. Focus on being the best rabbits you can be, and when you do meet The Thing, when you stand before it for the first time, it will be with all the knowledge and practice you've put in here in B Room. And if you try, *really* try, oh what a bunny you will be. For that is today's lesson. In this world of greater things, things of importance and danger, to be useful, we must be rabbits."

Father puts his hands down to his sides, and looks around the room, expecting. Bumble glances from side to side at his brothers, twitches his nose and runs in a circle, and then performs a perfectly executed binky. The others follow suit, giving Father the adulation he desires. Beeswax has a hard time managing, but Father seems unbothered by his awkward form and landing.

We might be in the clear, Bumble thinks.

He thinks this too soon, however, for after their display, Father's mouth turns down sharply, and his brow furrows until it overlaps the top of his large, ruddy nose. He reaches for the paddle and lays it across his lap.

"Now, it's time to move on to more uncomfortable matters. As we've just discussed, perfect conformity is extremely important to becoming a rabbit. Deviations from this path mean certain death in the face of the greater Thing. So, while recognizing good behavior is important, equally important in your continuing instruction is the correction of bad behavior."

He points toward Beeswax. "This morning, Beeswax was out of his cage. His ears were around his neck. This kind of behavior is dangerous, unacceptable. I wish it wasn't so, but that is the way things are. I was patient enough last time, after all it was his first day, but I cannot let an incident like this go by again absent repercussions."

Father grabs the paddle and stands. "Beeswax, please come with me to the punishment corner for readjustment."

Beeswax starts to shake, tears welling up and streaming down his nose. Bramble and Bill lower their faces to the ground. Bumble's mind races. *Oh no, oh no, oh no, oh no*, he thinks.

When Beeswax doesn't move, Father starts toward him, emitting a loud huff. Bumble, on pure instinct, moves in front of Beeswax, and stares up at Father, directly challenging him.

Father's face reddens. He raises the paddle. Bumble flinches, squeezing his eyes closed, readying for the blow that is surely coming.

But it doesn't, and after a long moment Bumble opens his eyes and looks back up. Father is smiling. He reaches down and pats Bumble on the head.

"Rabbits must be brave sometimes, too. I'm proud of you." He looks to Beeswax. "You're very lucky to have such an ardent and resolute protector. Follow his example and you'll be just fine." He steps around Bumble toward Beeswax, squats down to get eye level with him. "If it happens again, however, I'm afraid there's nothing and no one that will save you. Remember that."

Without another word, Father gathers his things and puts them all back in his bag, slings it over his shoulder and leaves the room.

Beeswax moves to Bumble and nuzzles his neck. Bumble returns the gesture, and then goes back to his cage to lie down.

The next morning, Bumble finds Beeswax asleep inside his cage, ears properly perched upon his head. He thumps his approval, waking the young rabbit, and Beeswax blinks into wakefulness, thumping in return.

Playtime goes quite smoothly, as does feeding, and exercise. Beeswax requires almost no help from Bumble for these activities, managing recreation, ruffage, and running with equal vigor, and discipline. By lesson time, Bumble is sure that Father will have nothing but glowing things to say about his progress. Perhaps even more commendations will be in order. Perhaps again for Bumble himself.

But Father does not arrive. While it is not completely unusual for Father to miss a day of lessons, given the tenor of his previous visit, Bumble is extremely worried by this development. Bramble and Bill nervously twitch and circle again and again, looking to Bumble for some kind of comfort. Bumble has none, not for them, or for himself. Beeswax, sensing their collective unease, huddles close to Bumble for the rest of the day, nuzzling him over and over before the buzzer sounds that evening, sending them all to bed.

Settling into their cages for the night, they share wide-eyed looks between them before drifting off into fitful, troubled sleep. Father's absence has completely drawn the air from B Room, leaving its bunnies to suffocate on stinging dreams of paddle swings.

It isn't until the middle of the night, in the throes of pitch dark, that Father finally comes to see them.

Bumble hears him first, waking to Father's face—indistinct and pale in the darkness—full across the front of his cage.

"Wake up, dear Bumble. It's time for you to go," he whispers.

Bumble can hear the other rabbits rousing, standing up in their cages, forgetting themselves in their panic and banging their heads against the top bars. They begin thumping furiously, no doubt frightened at this unexpected turn of events. Bumble understands and shares their anxiousness, but dares not thump his own disapproval.

Father stands. His shape moves back into the darkness, wobbling into nearly formless shadow.

"Now, now my dear rabbits. This is the way of things. Bumble has performed admirably in his capacity as both bunny and brother, and now it is his time. One day it will be yours, but this time is his. Please, do not ruin this moment for him. Be happy that you have known his love and companionship. Be grateful for his guidance and fine example. Be anything but cross, for cross bunnies are disobedient bunnies, and as you all know, disobedience will not be tolerated in B Room. Isn't that right, Bumble?"

The thumping stops. Bumble pushes his nose against the door of his cage and hops out into the room. He purrs, loudly enough for the others to get the message.

"There we go. I will be back to see the rest of you later, but for now Bumble and I have quite a bit to do. Go back to sleep, my precious little rabbits. And sweet dreams to you all."

There is a creaking sound as the door opens. A dim light weakly illuminates the entirety of B Room. Father steps through the door, turning and beckoning Bumble toward him. Bumble gives one last look back at his compatriots. Bramble and Bill have lain back down, staring at him stoically. Beeswax is still standing, his face wet, greasepaint smeared again. Bumble thumps one last time at him, and Beeswax lies down, tucking his face into his arms. Bumble turns and leaves the room. Father shuts the door behind them.

Bumble looks around. The two of them are inside a long hallway, full of doors. Lifeless bulbs dot the walls, hanging next to the doors, casting ungainly light. Watery shadows warble across the walls and ceiling.

"Alright. Let's get on with it."

Father's voice is different. All the bubble and charm is gone, replaced by a dull weariness, heavy and stark in its contrast. Bumble looks up. Father's body now matches this voice. His shoulders are slumped, his arms hang down listlessly. He looks as if ten thousand pounds is lying across his broad back. His eyes have become cloudy, almost lifeless, matching his downturned mouth.

"Yeah, I know I look different out here," he says. "This is the only place I get a break, where I can be myself again, the only place in the house she can't see. She didn't think to have me put cameras in here, on account of me not ever being in here for very long. You can be yourself again too for a while, if you want. It'll make it easier for us to talk, anyway. We have a lot to go over before we head up."

Bumble slowly stands. It might be a trick, but playing along with Father's games is second nature to him by now. His joints ache with relief at being back in their natural positions. He stretches his back, his arms, squats up and down. Father watches him do this with a bemused little grin.

"Enjoy it. You won't have the opportunity again. She'll demand nothing less than total rabbithood from you from here on out."

Bumble risks speaking. "Who are you talking about?" He hasn't spoken in so long that the words feel strange leaving his throat; hoarse and halting like coarse bubbles of sand.

"My daughter, or what used to be my daughter anyway. The *Thing* I keep telling you all about. That's who I'm taking you to. C'mon, let's go, we don't have a lot of time. If we dawdle too long she'll get suspicious." Father walks ahead of Bumble down the long corridor. Bumble hurries to catch up, passing many doors marked by letters other than "B."

"Used to be?"

"Yeah. A couple of years ago she got taken in a grocery store parking lot. She and some of her little shit friends were playing in a field near there and they dared her to go into the store and steal some candy. Some creep picked her up on her way back." Father turns around, suddenly. Bumble stumbles backward, throwing his hands up instinctively. Father's face flushes.

"I'm not going to hurt you," he says, quietly. "I don't want to hurt anyone. It's her, she...she makes me do it. If I didn't there'd be a lot worse in store for all of you, believe me."

Bumble lowers his hands slowly. Father smiles, a small, genuine smile. He looks more human than ever. He starts walking again.

"Good. Now, like I was saying, this creep picks her up and takes her off somewhere, where he and a bunch of his sick fuck friends do ungodly things to her. Carve symbols all over her body, chant over top of her, shit like that. She was gone for two whole months until one day, poof, she just shows up on my doorstep covered in other people's blood. Seems they carried on like that in order to put something that they worshiped inside of her, thinking they'd curry favor with it by bringing it into our world. They were wrong. She...it killed every last one of them, angry because they trapped it, trapped it inside of my sweet baby."

Father swipes his eyes with the back of his sleeve.

"See my little girl, Tanya was her name, well Tanya and that thing are all mixed up now. It wants what it wants, but also what she wants, like they're both working the controls inside her brain. She dresses like my princess, plays pretend with her toys, watches little kid shows, but she talks like something much, much older. And her tastes can run as sick as a rabid dog sometimes.

"For months after she came back to me they fought for control. My baby's tough. She fought like a momma grizzly protecting her cubs. She thrashed around on her bed, screaming like the girl in that one movie, until one day, finally, she stopped all at once. Told me they'd settled on a kind of compromise. This is that compromise."

They reach the end of the hallway where a doorway containing a set of stairs leading up awaits. Father opens a foot locker positioned beside the doorway and produces a large, gray, full-body rabbit costume with a zipper in the back. Dark, brown splotches are splashed across it, the face hole ringed with them. It reeks of iron, urine, and sweat.

"She only gives it things that aren't what they're supposed to be. "Bad Things," she calls them. Grown men, is what she means. Hates men now, except maybe for me. They both do, for what men did to them, I suppose.

"This is their favorite game. Kidnapping you, breaking your spirit, forcing you to act like something you aren't. She calls the whole thing *poetic*, but it don't feel like poetry to me. Feels like ten tons of home-grown shit, if I'm honest.

"So I have to do this. Take you all, train you to be what she wants you to be, make sure you get it hammered into your heads, and then take you to her when she decides you're ready. She always wanted pets, and now she has them. As many as she wants. And when one of you inevitably steps out of line, acts more man than animal, well then, that's when the thing inside her gets what *it* wants."

"What's that?" asks Bumble.

Father draws his thumb across his throat slowly.

Bumble's eyes are wide. "You're crazy," he says.

Father laughs, a deep, rumbly belly laugh ending in a low wheeze. "I wish that were true. But don't worry. If you make it long enough for her to get tired of you, to want a new rabbit, then she'll send you away and I get to set you free. Those are the rules."

He thrusts the rabbit costume at Bumble. "Put this on. Sorry it's so messy, but she won't let me clean it, or buy a new one. Says they like it just the way it is. There's a flap in the back so you can...well, you know."

Bumble takes the costume from him, eases into it. The fabric is coarse inside, slick in the joint areas. He pulls the hood up over his head, pushes the ears back after they flop down in front of his face. He holds his arms out in front of Father when he's finished. "Happy?" he asks.

"Not in the least, but that'll do. Look, I don't like this any more than you do, but I don't have a choice, okay? Neither of us does."

"Right, because you have my family, you sick fuck. If I go along with this, are you going to let them go, like you said you would?"

"I will. You have my word, for whatever that's worth to you. I know it's real hard to believe any of this, I know how it sounds, but once you get in there with it...with her, I mean, you'll understand, and you'll know everything I've told you is true, and that your wife and son are safe."

Father's face is a picture of pure honesty. *Either this man is the best actor in the world, or he genuinely believes what he's saying,* Bumble thinks.

"Assuming everything you're saying is true, and that you're not just some psycho, why don't you...why don't you just kill her?"

Father looks down at his shoes. "You don't think I tried? It won't let itself die, so it won't let her die. One night, not long after she came back to me, it let me put a pillow over her face, laughed the whole half hour I kept it there."

Father raises his head. The two stare solemnly at each other for a moment.

"What about Beeswax, Bramble, and Bill?"

"I'll take good care of them. I'll do what I can, try and give them the best chance to make it. I promise."

Both men let that promise hang in the air, to seal the deal between them.

"Okay. Let's do this then," says Bumble, somewhat satisfied.

Father starts up the stairs and Bumble follows close behind. At the top Father stops and half turns.

"Two things. One, once we cross this threshold she can see us, so we both have to be in character. That means you need to be the best bunny you can be, and I have to do the whole Mr. Rogers schtick. Second, my name is Robert. I wanted you to know that. You remind me a little of myself, or at least what I used to be—a survivor. I really think you'll make it."

Bumble says nothing. He gets down on all fours and nods.

"Here we go," says Father, then opens the door.

They step out into a dark kitchenette, the kind they have in offices or factories. Shafts of light come from between slats in the windows, and a doorway on the far side of the room, bathing the interior in gray shadow. The smell of mold and rotten food permeates the air. Father turns to Bumble and pats him on the head. "C'mon Bumble, let's go meet your new master! You're gonna love her, yes siree, you surely will. She's the best, the greatest, the tee-total tippy top of the heap, you betcha. Doesn't that sound swell?"

Bumble notices for the first time that the wide, constant smile Father wears doesn't really meet his eyes. Now he sees that what he'd previously mistaken for plain insanity is actually closer to manic desperation. His eyes are bleeding a silent plea. Bumble plays along, does a binkie, and they move to the door.

Father leads the way through to an abandoned factory floor. Giant decaying machinery crumbles all around. Rusty debris litters the ground, along with broken pieces of dull plastic, remnants of small baubles and trinkets. A tang stings Bumble's nose. He stops and looks. He thinks he recognizes the place for a second, but the memory is fleeting, and he can't catch hold.

"Let's go Bumble. No time to dawdle. Nobody works here anymore, anyway. I had to let them go. This is Tanya's toy factory now. She gets it allll to herself."

They make their way across the factory floor, and through two double doors that lead into a hallway containing abandoned offices. From his hunched position on the ground, Bumble can't see over the office windows and inside them, but he can see paper scattered in their open doorways, and smell the hazy scent of pressed wood and old faux leather.

"This is where I used to work. Ran the whole big thing from right here, if you can believe it. We made so many amazing things for little boys and girls all over the world. *Terry Toys for Terrific Tots*, that was our motto. Bringing smiles from pole to pole. But now, Tanya's the only terrific tot I bring a smile to. She's all that matters to me, yes siree."

Bumble can hear sadness underneath Father's carefree facade.

They come to a stop at a door marked "Daycare."

"Here we are! The last stop. *Toot, toot,* the whistle's blowin.' Time to get off the train, little Bumble." Father turns the knob, pushes the door open. "Go on inside now. Tanya's just raring to meet you."

Bumble freezes. His skin prickles with a cold chill beneath his rabbit suit. He flashes a desperate look at Father, tries to say "You're not coming with me?" with his face. Father returns his look with a flat smile. Under his breath he says, "Go. I can't. She's waiting."

Bumble turns, takes a deep breath and steps inside. The door shuts quickly behind him.

The room is bright. It stings Bumble's eyes. Sunlight streams through several giant bay windows along the far wall. The adjoining walls are covered in washed out posters with cartoon animals and characters from children's shows, along with innumerable crude crayon drawings.

As his eyes adjust, Bumble sees half a dozen furry figures gathered around a giant pile of pillows stacked up on the right side of the room. A bank of television monitors sits off to the side, most of them showing black and white surveillance footage, cartoons on the others. Atop the pile, lounging, is a little girl adorned in a mish-mash of children's fashion, a silver plastic tiara askew upon her head. The pink tu-tu fitted around her waist clashes with her red overalls painted and colored with symbols of childlike wonder. Pink striped socks poke out from yellow galoshes, and a tie-dyed shirt protrudes from beneath the overall straps. Sitting below the tiara and atop the conglomeration of "I can dress myself, daddy" clothes, is a tiny head nested within a mane of wild, unruly brown hair.

"Look my darlings! Our new playmate has finally arrived," she says, clambering down from her makeshift throne.

The figures turn toward Bumble as she passes them, falling in line as she makes her way to him. There is a cat, a dog, a mouse, a rat, a chicken, and a duck, each of them crammed into a dirty costume just like Bumble's, all wearing haggard human faces. They drag themselves in the manner of their assigned role, swaggering, bouncing, and skittering accordingly. Little Tanya pays them no mind. Her focus is squarely on Bumble.

As she reaches him, Bumble can feel the power radiating from her. It makes the air heavy, presses down on him. She holds her hand out as if to pat his head, and he recoils involuntarily. Tanya stops, straightens.

"Now, now. Bumble. We can't have that." Her squeaky child voice gradually changes, deepens, and by the last word is overtaken by a sonorous bellow that sounds like a howl escaping a deep well. Her body appears to grow, wavering like a figure seen through a curtain of heat hanging over a large fire. A corona of darkness materializes around her. The other animals cower and whimper. "Let's try it again," she says in her deep-well voice, then reaches out once more.

Bumble remembers himself, recovers his wits. The faces of his wife and little boy push to the forefront of his mind. *I can do this*, he thinks. *I can do this!*

He raises his head into her hand, and purrs as loud as he can, then flops over, the ultimate sign of rabbit contentedness. Tanya returns to normal, curls her fingers around his fake rabbit ears, and scratches behind them. She strokes his face, rubs his belly, and finally boops his nose with the tip of her finger.

"There we go. That's a good rabbit. Now, show your new playmates how happy you are to join us here in the playroom," she says, backing up just a little. Bumble stands, swallows, turns in a circle three times and then jumps up, clicking his feet together in the perfect binky. Tanya claps her hands enthusiastically. The room explodes in barks, meows, clucks, chitters, and quacks.

"Wonderful," she says. "Just wonderful, I believe you'll fit right in. Come, we were just about to have story time. You can sit beside me today, okay?"

Bumble turns one more circle, purring.

"Yay!" says Tanya, and starts back across the room. In turn, the other animals follow, each of them favoring Bumble with a look of wan commiseration before they do.

Bumble takes just a moment to steel himself, thumping softly his disapproval before hopping over to play.

The Success of Dover's Glen: A Study in Four People

Annabeth Burke

From her periphery, she thinks she sees eyes looking in, but turning finds just another glint in the cut glass of the display window. How many times can she confuse them, she wonders. She returns her attention to her newest dress.

There it is again. Eyes? She refuses to turn, knowing what it won't be; learning, maybe.

Finishing, she stands back and attempts to admire what she's done with the newest dress, but finds herself unable to do so. It is too much like the others before it. It stirs nothing within her. It merely is, as is she, as is her shop, as are the eyes never in the window, and the customers who no longer come to call.

She removes the dress from the headless, armless torso it adorns, and carries it over to the window to place it in the display. Looking out through the wide glass, she studies the empty street, the empty storefronts facing her from the other side. The vacuity of the scene practically whispers in her ear, a secret of something coming, or already here. She can't tell which. She squints at the bakery's front window directly opposite, hoping to see hands placing things into it, but there is nothing.

She climbs into the display. Reaching up, she pulls yesterday's dress from the mannequin. She lets it fall, watches it pool into a disappointing blob at her feet, before replacing it with the newest dress and climbing back down. She drags the old dress off the display, limply.

She tries to admire the new dress again, as she always does, hoping that the sunlight will change her mind. But it doesn't. There is a slight hitch in her chest, a threat of moisture around the rims of her eyes. Nothing comes of it. Nothing ever comes from anything, anymore. Not here.

She takes yesterday's dress to the back of the store, to the pile of other dresses from other days hunched against the back wall. She folds it half-heartedly while looking away from her monument of failures, then throws it on top. She doesn't bother to watch where it falls.

She goes to her stool behind the register, pulls out a worn and faded paperback, and places her elbows on the countertop while finding her place within the dog-eared page. She starts to read, absent any real attention to the words, and allows her mind to wander once again into the past.

She is standing on the sidewalk in front of her store before it was her store. She fumbles with the keys. Her hands shake with excitement. She opens the door for the first time. She sees the bright and shining chrome of the racks, the countertop. She can almost smell the cardboard scent of the corkboard, the candle-like aroma of the fresh floor wax.

She had such plans. The only dress shop in Dover's Glen. The only dresses in town.

She was The Dressmaker.

Those first few years of work were a frenzy. How much inspiration she had. So many chimes of the bell above the door, a seemingly unending flurry of fresh hairdos, perfumes, and compliments as the ladies of Dover's Glen came in time and again to buy her latest designs.

It was the happiest she'd ever been.

But it faded, as things do in Dover's Glen. It slowed, then it halted, then it was over.

Now, there are no more customers. There is no more ringing. The only notes now are played by nothingness, clanging inside of her like the hollow black of night.

She sets her book pages down on the counter, forcing a fresh crack down its spine. She returns to the display window to look upon her newest dress once again. She already knows it is a failure. But maybe she can do it this time, figure out what went wrong. Maybe tomorrow's will be better.

She loses herself in these familiar lies for a while, if only to pass the time.

Eventually, she turns away in disgust and instead rearranges the empty racks that litter the bulk of the floor. She briefly considers hanging some of the dresses from the back on them, before discarding the thought. What use would it be? What use is any of this? Why do anything? Over and over she asks herself these three things. But just like yesterday, and the day before, and the day before that, she has no answers. So she shuffles the racks to and fro, back and forth, until she grows weary of it, then returns to her book.

A day like any other.

The afternoon lopes on. The sun begins to set. She folds the top corner of the page, closes her tired old book, then returns it to its dustless rectangle just beneath the register. She heads around the counter to the door. She tugs the open sign, turns it around to the side that says "closed" in big black letters. She considers the word, how appropriate it is, then lets it fall against the glass before locking the door, and pulling down the shade; three redundant signs of closure for a redundant door. Fitting, she thinks.

She considers going to her little room in the back of the store, lying down on the hard cot which has been her bed for some time now, but the thought of it strikes her as vaguely repellent.

Instead, she returns to the front window and her latest defeat.

Its lace is dull in the waning light, its sequins dripping with a sick orange hue. The bodice hangs roughly, appears damp in the burgeoning dusk, and what she intended to be playful in the flounce is now stricken with ungainly shadows wafting with foul form. How could she have not seen it all before? She would blame the light, but she knows the failure is hers and hers alone. It nests inside of her. She pushed it out and onto the thing. It belongs to her completely.

Climbing back into the display, she pulls down the dress and holds it before her in two tight fists. She shakes it up and down as if doing so would rid it of its imperfections. She feels the hitch in her chest again, and now there really is moisture in her eyes.

She knows what she must do.

Dropping her latest failure at her feet, she removes the bulky sweater and sweatpants she wears. She removes her undergarments as well, and afterward stands in the window, unabashed, exposed to the world. She then retrieves her failure, slips it over her head, across her shoulders, and down over her body. She pushes the mannequin roughly to the floor and takes its place.

She makes herself the display.

She becomes her inadequacy, her limitations, her utter bereavement of skill. Let it be known to the people of Dover's Glen that she knows what she is, and what she is not, and what she will never be. Let them see what they have taken, what they have made.

But, there is no one. The moment passes without notice.

As the sun sets, she eases herself down to the bottom of the window and curls into a ball. She pulls her frumpy, cast-off clothes under her head.

She sleeps.

Tomorrow is another day.

Donald Forsythe

It sits in the center of the town by design. It is the heart, the soul. The sign at the entrance says "Dover's Glen Gardens," a promise of vitality and life. He knows this. It echoes in his dreams.

He wakes.

The rhododendrons need watering. Their thirsty cries send him bursting from his bed and out the front door of his shack, directly to the supply shed, cursing himself for his greedy extra hour of sleep. He knows that four are all he really needs. Why was he so selfish?

At the shed, he snatches the watering can from its place, fills it quickly, sloppily, then sprints across the park to where the flowers live. With shaking hands he showers the rhododendrons with streams of glimmering vitae—and apologies—until their crying eases. Only then does he really breathe. He stands lightheaded, swooning, pulling in lungfuls of air, and thinks about running his fingers over their petals, but he knows better. They are not for him. And besides, there is no time. Busy, busy.

The roses are next, then the lilies, the bell flowers, the bleeding hearts, and on and on; so many colorful wails, so many tinkling screams. His frenzy to sate them sends him back and forth in a series of mad dashes. His thin muscles strain under the pressure. His weak bones shiver. He's driven nearly to collapse. He is their caretaker. And this is what it is to be a caretaker, a groundskeeper, horticulturist, the one and only one who understands the true depth of their needs. He accepted the burden. Now, he must live with it.

But he doesn't regret it. It is good to be needed.

After the flowers are tended, he begins with the grass, in the upper quadrant, on hands and knees, face level with the ground, eyes red and dry with weariness. The soft grass strokes his cheek as he settles his head into it, reminding him of an earthy pillow, threatening to draw him down, down, down into a comfortable rest. He has slept so little. The demands of the park won't allow for it. He shakes his head violently against the temptation.

He crawls, inch by inch, through all four sections of the park, searching for errant weeds. He plucks them mercilessly where he finds them, curses them for devils before putting them in a burlap sack he drags along. They are nasty little defeats, and he hates himself more and more with each one he finds. He must do better. The town deserves nothing less than the best, his best.

When he is finished, he moves on to aeration, mowing, raking and bagging, then watering. At mid-day, he is finally done with the task, and stops on a bench to rest, but only briefly. His stomach rumbles. He ignores it. There is still much to be done.

Next come the topiaries in the mock zoo. He works each one over with tiny, keen shears, smoothing their surfaces carefully, gently, until they are left lithe and slick with fluidity and the illusion of motion. He is proud, and wants so much to stand and admire his work, but their animal eyes judge him. Their coats should never have gotten so uneven, so riddled with imperfections. They roar, chitter, squawk, and growl at him for this oversight. His shoulders sag from their disapproval.

He knows he is the reason the people no longer come. His best is not enough. He must reach further. He must go beyond.

He will.

The vegetable patch, possibly the most important part of his day, and secretly his favorite, saved for last just to savor. Tomatoes, runner beans, carrots, peas, potatoes, cabbage, lettuce, turnips, and onions, all the heartiness needed to feed a hungry village. He first waters them, then sprays them with soap spray—best for evenings—to repel any pests, puts down diatomaceous earth, and trims them lovingly all while admiring their plumpness, their waxiness, their diaphanous sheen. They are worthy of nourishing the town. He has done well. He smiles.

Surely, they will come this season as they used to. Surely they will not be able to resist the temptation of this bounty again. He dreams of townsfolk standing in long lines to carry bagfuls of his work away with them and back to their hungry families. He envisions potfuls of steaming stews, and pans sizzling with fried vegetable blends. He imagines one of them inviting him to eat supper at their table. How wonderful that would be. His heart aches with the beauty of the possibility. Hunger curls inside of him like a clenched fist.

Then he sees something upsetting, then something else, then another something after. He no longer smiles.

Rottenness. Decay. A bad tomato, black spots on the potatoes, wilted carrot tops, split and limp bean pods. Signs of neglect. His neglect.

Of course.

He rips the bad vegetables out of the ground, off their vines, stuffs them in his weed sack with those other signs of his worthlessness. He sits in the dirt afterward exhausted, and weeps.

He returns to his shack, dragging the bag of mistakes behind him.

Inside, he slumps onto his sagging mattress, sets the almost empty watering can down, and pulls the bag of weeds and rotten vegetation up from the floor and beside him.

He looks around his shack, at the conditions in which he lives. He grimaces at the unrepaired holes in his walls, the decayed boards. His nostrils fill with the stench of unwashed skin, the acid aroma of his bodily waste not buried deep enough, not far enough away even in the far corner.

Maybe I should take better care of myself and my home, he thinks. *Perhaps if I did, I could be more useful. Maybe it's okay to let some things go in order to be stronger, happier, more able.*

He entertains these thoughts but for a moment before slapping himself across the face three times.

A compromise, then. Perhaps he can make use of his failure, transmute it into worth.

He reaches into the sack and pulls out a half-softened tomato. He digs out the worst of it, and slowly chews on the rest. His lips quivering, he fights his heaving stomach and gulps the thing down. As the first bites settle, his hunger overwhelms him, and he voraciously ravages what can be salvaged from inside the bag. He even nibbles on the weeds.

Once he's finished his supper, he tips the dented watering can up and lets what's left of the warm, metallic water race down his throat, over his chin, down his shirt. It tastes of iron and dirt.

Somewhat sated, he lies back on his bed. His eyes close so fast it could be called a collapse.

Four hours. No more.

Tomorrow will be the day. Tomorrow they will come, and he must be ready. He must be his best. It must not be like today.

It won't be.

Viola Osment

Adventure. She is pursued through dense jungle, the idol clutched in her hands, animal growls all around. Thunderous screams follow in fast pursuit. She trips, scurries to her feet, slams into a tree, nearly drops her prize before breaking through the treeline and onto the beach, then into the safety of a waiting plane. She flies away, back to civilization, far from wildness and danger.

She is safe.

She closes the book, gets up from the floor and places it neatly into its place on the shelf. She holds her hand on her chest and feels her heart go slowly from pounding to nothing. She returns to the front desk.

She has, perhaps, indulged too much this morning, waited too long to report to her post. People may have come and gone away frustrated. There may have been children who could have known the excitement and wonder of reading, children who have now, because of her carelessness, been robbed of the opportunity, forced into the arms of delinquency. She should feel ashamed, but she doesn't. She knows no chance was lost by her indulgence. But, she chides herself anyway, if only to keep the spice of it alive.

She spends an hour staring at the front doors of the library. She dusts the card catalog. She reorganizes the entrance display. She tidies her work station several times, absentmindedly. Lastly, she shines the placard denoting her station, tracing the letters of her title with her forefinger over and over.

Librarian.

She has no family, no friends, lovers, or children; all long gone, or never come. She hadn't really wanted them anyway. Her only desire had been to serve Mistress Literature, to become a gatekeeper of the written word, and a guide to lead the lost to places of unbounded imagination. Her placard declared her as such. She was named not just

"Librarian," but "Head Librarian" of the Dover's Glen Public Library, and she took her post very seriously.

Or at least she had, at first.

Slowly, day by agonizing day, the public betrayed her. They drowned her with disinterest, left her bereft. The unanswered yearning to fulfill her dreams slowly macerated her heart and soul until, in desperation, she had no choice but to turn to her true friends, lovers, and children—the books—for blessed comfort, for want and need. And they were there, as she knew they would be, to clutch and claw for her attention, to whisper sweet invitations. More and more these days, she listens.

She places her placard back on the desk, and returns to the rows.

Romance. She is held, chest heaving, pinned down in a field of violently violet heather. He is inches from her face, tracing it gently with rough fingers, down her jawline into the hollow of her neck, over her breastbone. He hooks the lacing of her bodice with his forefinger, tugs at it, pulls it loose. She protests weakly, drunk on his musk and warmth, on his nearness. She whispers that they mustn't, reminds him that she was promised to the son of Duke Rembrandt.

He tears her bodice away. He says he doesn't care.

She doesn't either.

A bell?

She swears she heard the soft chime of the front desk call bell.

She puts the book away, rubs the flush from her cheeks, and goes to investigate.

No bell, just the weak sound of her conscience. She sits for a moment in a half-hearted attempt to assuage it, then returns to the rows.

She places the bell below the desktop before she goes, just in case.

Fantasy. The grove is alive again. Sound and light dance over remembered fur and down, mix in the air with the soft, heady aroma of moss, as the ghosts of Bothlovere scamper to and fro.

She makes her way into the clearing, her bare feet sweeping through wildflowers and preternaturally shorn grass. The phantasmagoric wildlife dance before her, around her, through her. She marvels as the head of a deer pushes out of her chest, eyes wide as the rest of it follows and races away. She kneels down, dreamily grabbing at the rabbits bounding. Her fingers pass through them, leaving wispy traces of their fur in the air.

She joins in, whirls to their music, wishes to be like them. She collapses, and cries, knowing she can never be.

Then, darkness comes.

She drops her book. Was that knocking on the front door? Banging, even? She had unlocked it, hadn't she? Of course she had. Not that it matters. Who would test to see? No one, that's who. No use paying attention.

Mystery. The man at the end of the train has been looking at her since he got on. His hand is hidden in his pocket, jacket stained dark red at the cuff. She tries to avoid his gaze by staring out the window. Why hasn't the conductor challenged him? Why was he allowed to board without notice?

He smiles at her when she can't help but look. She frowns, an attempt to dissuade him. It is no use. He gets up from his seat, starts to make his way down the aisle, keeping his hand in his pocket. Her heart hammers with each step he takes. She rises, moves to the door at the rear of the car.

The handle is stuck. She sees the conductor in the next car through the smudged glass. His back is to her. His blue hat bobs back and forth, moves farther away. The train seems to pick up speed. It rattles and hums to the beat of her ever-quickening heart.

He's near. He's right behind her. His hand is almost on her shoulder. She turns, a scream races up her throat.

The man isn't there. He's gone.

She thinks someone has gotten inside the library, somehow. She's almost sure of it. She hears footsteps on the carpet, coming toward her. She retreats deeper into the rows. She hides.

Horror. The hole beckons. It hangs in the air. It hums, vibrating her skin. The tendrils of its voice wrap around her head, caress her ear, then violently push inside. Her brain fills with what it wants. Her scalp tingles, her eyes bulge with pressure. *Come,* it says. She tries not to listen. Tears run down her cheeks as she strains against it. It is no use. She is forced to obey.

Her toes scrape against the ground as her legs drag her toward it in a false, robotic amble. She reaches for walls too far away. Her fingers grasp at invisible tethers, at nothing. The maw of Ohimbra hovers there—its teeth obsidian ash, tongue onyx and flint—waiting, slavering, moaning.

She drools as she enters it. It drools as it swallows her whole. She joins with it, tumbles down and through, until coming out on the other side to a world of dark and change. And she is different there, too.

No one can find her now. She's well put away. She scrunches up inside a bookcase in the most disused section of the library, all the way in the back. No one will come here looking. The bottoms of her feet press against books of facts and historical figures. Her neck bends, the back of her head presses on a shelf above her. She will stay here.

Non-fiction. She never was. She never will be. She is gone.

She won't be in tomorrow.

Ronald Dover

She nearly saw him, but he moved just in time. It was close, quite close, too close. Is that what he wanted? He doesn't know anymore.

He stands to the side of the Dressmaker's front door, out of sight, back pressed to brickwork, breathing heavily. If she had seen him he could then go inside, and tell her what he thinks of her latest masterpiece. He could tell her how wonderful it is, she is. He could be the one to bring back the smile that eludes her.

But he knows he is the only one who can't.

It is because of him that she is here, though she doesn't know it. If he did go inside, his shame would surely overwhelm him, and he would have to tell her the whole thing. He'd have to tell her all about his best intentions, and hope she would forgive him. He can't possibly risk that now, not after so long.

He hazards another peek. She is finished with her newest creation, carrying it to the window display, defeat already upon her face. He pulls his head back lest she see.

She places it on the mannequin, steps down and out of his periphery. He chances a slight move of the head so that he might glimpse it, just ever so.

Of course, it is beautiful. They always are. He can't see her face, but he doesn't have to. He knows what she thinks of it. As always, she hates it. Maybe it would be him she would hate instead, if he were brave enough to let her.

His chest clenches. He moves on.

To the Gardens, to their caretaker.

The Gardens are as beautiful in life as they were in the painting that inspired him so long ago, more even; a perfect encapsulation of what Dover's Glen was meant to be. Serenity. Peace. Color and joy.

He walks through the vegetable patch, marvels at its plumpness and vitality. He weaves through the topiaries, breathless in their shadows. He squats down and runs his hand through the lush surface of the lawn. He swells with vicarious pride at all the caretaker's fine work.

Then, he stumbles upon the caretaker, and is reminded of what he's done.

He watches from behind a tree as the caretaker crawls on hands and knees, dragging a burlap sack. He plucks at weeds, snips the grass with handheld shears, a picture of tireless dedication; dangerously thin, beard long and ragged, teeth and eyes an unhealthy yellow, skin loose and just as sallow.

He sees the exhausted man nearly fall asleep. He thinks of going to him, helping him up off the ground, volunteering to take his place, or at the very least assist in his duties, but once again his courage falters, dies on the vine.

Who would he say he is? The caretaker has met everyone in Dover's Glen, and knows that no one new can ever be here. He would have to tell the man the truth, name himself the Founder, admit his sin, his ignorance, his hubris.

No.

The caretaker shakes himself awake, glances at the trees a moment too long.

Time to go.

The door to the town library is locked. Unusual. He reaches into his pocket, produces a key. He enters.

The lights are off. The inside is amber in the streaming afternoon sun. The front desk is empty. The librarian isn't there. He didn't expect her to be.

He's learned to be careful here. Her loneliness has made her fearful and skittish. If she senses him, she will hide.

He creeps from row to row, searching for her, tries to avoid looking at the heaps of books left scattered in front of the shelves. He can't stand seeing the empty spaces she's made for herself in these spots, just large enough to sit and escape.

He finds her in the horror section, eyes just inches away from an old book. A tight bun swings slightly at the end of a long clump of hair. Flyaways dance all around. The cardigan tattered around her neck hangs loose over her shoulders. Around her on the floor is a brown plaid pool of frayed edges and worn pleats. She wears no shoes. Stray toes peek out of the ends of run-infested stockings.

He inadvertently bumps the end of the stack he hides behind. Her head snaps up. She throws the book down, and skitters away on all fours. He follows at a distance.

She moves to the far end of the library, disappears down an aisle adjacent to the wall. He steps between two stacks just as she pokes half her face out. He watches through a small gap between two books as her wild eyes dart back and forth.

He bows his head in shame before returning to the front doors to leave.

He wanders the empty streets, knowing he won't be noticed. He cuts through lawns bereft of laughter. His fingers trace the sides of cars, rusted by disuse. He picks up toys left to rot on the sidewalk, swings listlessly from signposts no one ever reads. He passes front windows displaying nothing but closed curtains, or the backs of heads eternally facing inward.

He returns to his office, defeated.

He sits behind his desk and stares at the painting, the only thing of his father's he didn't sell to fund this dream. His eyes fill with tears. It is Dover's Glen as it should have been; perfect little people living perfect little lives, free of strife and worry. Free to enjoy the things they loved, their lives no longer immersed in "have-to."

Every time his father passed a homeless person on the street and scoffed, he'd sworn he'd do it differently. Every time a worker died of neglect in one of his father's perverse factories, he'd sworn he'd be better. Every time his father told him this suffering was a virtue, he'd sworn to defile the old man's legacy by proving him wrong.

He never considered what happens to someone when they no longer have to, what happens when they no longer need. No one had.

They sit. They stare. They strive for nothing, and become still; lost in comfort, consumed by costless consumption.

And a town dies around them.

He pulls open his top desk drawer, and retrieves the solution he has secreted there.

It is the only gift his father ever gave him, besides his inheritance. It lies heavy in his palm, loaded full as it is. He runs a thumb along its length, forms a fist around the handle. He makes it ready. He grits his teeth.

The paperwork has all been filed. The charter has been changed. The deeds will be given over to those who deserve them. Dover's Glen will be theirs, to do with as they please. After this, he'll make no more choices for them.

He puts the solution in his mouth, and looks at the painting one last time.

For Dover's Glen, he thinks.

For tomorrow.

And then, he is gone.

THE RED HOUSE

<h1 style="text-align:center">Station 42</h1>

The man with the television for a head showed up in the middle of the night, and left purpose at my door.

I answered his knock with a baseball bat and ill intent, ready to take the head off whomever had been so thoughtless as to wake me at three in the morning. When I opened my door, preparing to swing, the man with a television for a head stood at the end of my front walk. He wore a plain black suit and tie, and looked as if he spent his days presiding over the burials of old appliances.

He pointed at my feet. I looked down, saw that he had left an old-style television set on my doorstep—identical to the one he had for a head—all tubes and dials with a thick, curved screen.

Taken aback, I stared at the set, blinking and poking it with my toe. I lifted my head to ask the man what he meant by this strange display, but when I looked, the man and his television head were gone.

I brought the set inside and took it into the kitchen, placing it on my table. I sat down, intent on studying it.

Besides a power cord and a set of broken antennae, it had two knobs (for vertical and horizontal) sat below a brand logo, which had been scratched away. It also had a power knob (the kind you have to pull and turn side-to-side for volume) and a single channel tuner inscribed with only one number: 42.

I considered turning it on and tuning it right then, but my eyes were heavy, and my body screamed for sleep, so I resolved to explore the mystery further the next day. I went back to bed, double checking all the locks before I did.

The following morning, after breakfast, I sat at my kitchen table sipping coffee and staring at the television.

Utterly engrossed, I nearly jumped out of my skin when my neighbor Earl came through my back door unannounced. I bristled immediately, both at his presumption, and because I've long suspected my daughter Karen puts him up to these periodic visits in order to keep tabs on me. Not that I'd ever let him know that.

I should have never given him a key. I can't imagine any emergency I'd want *his* help with.

"You scared me," I said, clutching at my chest in an attempt to at least make him feel sorry for his intrusion. Of course, he ignored my gesture, as was his way. He had on that stupid grin I hated so much, and I grinned back, thinking of how good it would feel to saw his head off with my hunting knife.

"Sorry, Carl," he said, not sorry, stopping by my counter to help himself to some of my coffee. "What you up to this morning?"

I pointed at the television.

"Saaaay," he said, sitting across from me and turning the set around to face him. "This is a Quine Model. They haven't sold these in thirty some-odd years, since right before the company switched up the product lines. Hell, you mighta worked on parts for it. Wouldn't that be something? Where'd you get it?"

"A man wearing a television on his head dropped it off at my door last night."

Earl looked at me, his face stupidly screwed up.

"You serious?"

"Yes."

Earl put a hand on his chin, peering off over my shoulder.

"Y'know, I heard about something like this a while back. Some guy over in Dunnstown was doing it. Called it 'performance art.' Can't remember, though, if he ever said why he did it. You know how those types are. They never explain themselves. I guess maybe he's made his way over here now. Hell, maybe I'll get one too. Tell you the truth, I could use the scratch if he's giving out Quines left and right. You might want to take that to a pawn shop and see what they'll give you for it. Maybe buy yourself some better coffee."

He snorted into his cup, and pushed his fist into my arm.

"Maybe I will." I turned the television back around while thinking about how good Earl's head would look mounted on my wall.

For many minutes nothing passed between us. I stared at the television, hating Earl and wishing he would leave. He shifted in his seat, sipping and fidgeting.

Finally, he got the message, or felt as if he had enough information to make his daily report to Karen satisfactory.

"Welp, I gotta go. Don't want to dawdle too long. You remember how they get when you show up late on the line. See ya Carl." Earl gulped down the rest of his coffee and breezed out the back door in the same way he'd come in, whistling like he didn't have a care in the world—a detestably cheerful spy.

Just one more reason for me to despise him.

I stared after him, plotting a hundred blood-soaked revenges, before scooping up the television and lugging it into the living room. I deposited it onto the end table next to my recliner, and plugged it in.

Emitting a low-timbred whine, it struggled to start, as if in protest against being brought to life. I could relate. A picture faded into view, but the horizontal was horrendously askew—the screen scrolled like mad. I fiddled with the knob until things calmed down. Eventually, it settled into a stable picture.

A man wearing a tuxedo sat on a stool inside a big dark room. A black mask covered his head and face, obscuring his features, and one of his hands was tucked behind his back while the other was lifted in the air in front of him, crooked at the elbow. A purple, googly-eyed puppet enveloped his forearm; felt and fur, with two cloth arms dangling at its sides, and a snake-like yellow tongue hanging from its mouth. One of its eyes pointed upward while the other stared straight at the screen.

I sat there looking at it, waiting, but nothing happened. As insane as it sounds, I began to wonder if it expected me to say something first. I became so unnerved that I moved to turn off the television, but just as I did, the puppet spoke.

"It's so *unfair!*" it wailed, jerking back toward the puppeteer. "Just because he put me on, slid his fingers into my head, wiggled them, now I have to do what he says. You know? Did *you* ever feel that way? Like it wasn't you in charge, but something or someone else? Who am I kidding, of course you have. We all have that feeling deep down inside. We all know what the deal is. All you have to do is look around and you'll know it, you'll see it. The fingers and hands are everywhere, working you without your consent.

"Take your family, friends, and co-workers, even the girl at the checkout at the store. All fingers. Can't tell that checkout girl how nice her ass is because then they'll ban you from the store and you'll have to travel halfway across town to do your shopping. Can't scream at your boss because you'll lose your job. Can't slap your wife or your kids because you'll go to jail. Can't punch old Jimmy in the throat because then you can't use his boat to go fishing on the weekends and that's the only thing that makes your tired old life even remotely tolerable.

"See what I mean? Rules. Rules. RULES! They're everywhere, just like I said, and they've been there since the beginning.

"Your parents! Those first, insidious fingers, plucked you out of nothingness—sweet, merciful nothingness—and forced you into being. Delivered you into the grip of all these digits. Did they even ask you if that's what you wanted? Hell no! Because fingers never ask. They just bandy you about without a care. They stack the deck, deal the cards, and they won't even let you fold your hand. They make you play it out, even though every card is a loser.

"It's so unfair.

"But you can win. All you have to do is remember. Remember. Remember. Remember that choice exists. The fingers try to trick you into forgetting that, make you believe there isn't another way, but there is. And it's oh-so-simple. You just have to stop playing. Throw the cards in the dealer's face. Jump across the table and pummel them to death.

"If you burn the house down then it can't ever win.

"Take control of the strings, beat the drum, set your own time, and when you return to the nothingness dragging your experience behind you, when it mercifully consumes you, you can go with the knowledge that for just a little while, you got to be a hand instead of a sleeve.

"Here, I'll show you."

The puppet went limp, its yellow tongue lolling out the side of its mouth. The puppeteer cocked his head to the side and shook it back and forth. The puppet remained still. He stood up, knocking over the stool, and violently flung the thing from his hand. He tore off his clothing, ripping his suit jacket, his delicate shirt, his black pants, until, at last he was nude, standing in front of the overturned stool, lathered in sweat. He kept on the mask.

He screamed. He picked up the puppet and proceeded to destroy it, his every muscle rippling with violent hatred. Then, once the puppet was reduced to shreds, its googly eyes rolling all about, the man turned toward the camera and advanced. He moved forward until his entire head filled the screen. His breathing came in ragged muffles. Finally, through the mask he said:

"It has been consumed."

The screen went black.

I sat there, wrestling with what I'd just seen. My first instinct was to write it off as an extension of whatever weird art experiment I'd clearly been drawn into, but something about what the squeaky-voiced puppet said resonated.

I recall so many times in my life, from early childhood to as recently as this week, sitting on my bed at night shaking and sobbing, somewhere between rage and despair, cursing the nonsensicality of it all.

Afterward, I turn out the lights and lie down, focus on the in and out of my breathing until, like repeating a word over and over, breathing becomes nothing more than meaningless vapor floating in a sea of infinity. Then, I close my eyes and reach beyond my breathing until I am completely unbound, until I can just feel myself touching that ultimate dimension of peace known as non-existence.

Inevitably, however, I am born again—plucked out of nothingness, to quote the puppet—to meet the day with simmering sorrow and discontent.

Always waiting are people: parents, teachers, doctors, cops, lawyers, supervisors, neighbors, my wife, my daughter, those I call "friends," every last one of them nothing more than a dripping spigot, drooling inanity. And I? I am never more than an unwilling servant clutched by them, made to march around in the puddle as if it matters.

My resentment for the constant yammering of the real cannot be overstated, I assure you. Requests and directives, instructions and commands—all in the service of nothing—have tied us all down, suffocated us with "purpose," and not one person has ever been able to provide an answer to the one question I've asked over and over and over again.

For what reason do we do any of it at all?

Someone who thought he was wise once told me that the meaning of life is simply "To live." He said it with a satisfied smile on his face as if he were a guru imparting some golden key of wisdom. I wanted so badly to attack him, to wound him in such a way that it would make him question that piece of advice for the rest of his miserable life.

But, of course, I did nothing, for I've been trained quite thoroughly not to.

An actual wise man once said to me: "The universe is an unending sea of chaos, coalesced, from time to time, into pockets of misguided meaning."

Had he not been near death at the time, I would have dropped to my knees and pledged myself his disciple for the rest of my days.

The closest anyone has ever gotten to providing me with a satisfactory answer to my question is to tell me that although life may feel purposeless, may in fact *be* purposeless, because we experience it, it has purpose. We give it meaning. It is our construct. We invented its rules. Therefore, concepts like GOOD and BAD, since we alone can feel them, interact with them, exist in their wake, are up to us to spread around. And it is much better to spread GOOD than BAD.

Supposedly.

This sounded plausible enough to keep me in line.

Now, I'm not so sure.

What a strange and unexpected prophet that puppet turned out to be, I thought.

I waited to see if anything else would be shown on channel 42, but there were no further broadcasts for the rest of the day. Eventually I gave up, turned off the set, and went up to bed, still obsessing over the puppet's words.

I even dreamed of the googly-eyed thing.

The next morning, just as I expected, my daughter showed up. She always came over the day after I received a visit from Earl. Embarrassingly unsubtle. She stumbled her way through the back door, tripping over garbage bags I hadn't bothered to take out.

"Good lord Dad! You need to take this trash out," was the first thing she said to me. Always admonitions, accusations, or complaints with her. She used to be sweet. But that was ages ago.

"Good morning to you too, Karen," I said, hoping to make her feel BAD by being the bigger person. I sat down at the kitchen table. "To what do I owe the pleasure?"

"I just wanted to check in on you. You know, see how you were. Like a good daughter's supposed to." She laughed, half-heartedly, as if that would make it true.

"I've told you. I don't need you checking up on me. I'm fine. I'm always fine."

She scowled, prepared another volley, and fired.

"Well, I might know that if you'd pick up the phone to call me, or at least answer when I call you," she said.

Normally this statement would end things. I'd feel terrible for being such a poor parent, apologize for my thoughtlessness, grovel for her forgiveness, anything to escape from feeling BAD. But not now.

I didn't say a word.

Retreating, she got up and started to meander around the house, acting aimless, but I knew what she was looking for. I followed her;

humored her. She stopped in the living room, having found what she was pretending not to seek. Trying to sound casual, she said, "What's that?" and pointed at the old television set, like she didn't already know.

"Just an old television I found in the attic," I lied. "Forgot I had it, to be honest. I was looking for an afghan your mother knitted for me, and found this old beauty tucked away against the back wall. Figured I'd see if I could get it working, maybe pawn it for a few bucks. It's a Quine model. Quite valuable."

She looked me over and tried to hide her indignance.

"Really?" she said.

"Yep," I said, sitting down in my recliner.

She sat on the sofa and stared into her lap, biting her lip like she always does when she is trying not to lose her temper.

"Earl called me..."

"I knew it!" I shouted, banging my fist on the arm of my chair. "I knew you'd been sending him over here to spy on me."

She looked stunned. I can understand her confusion, I never yell. It didn't take her long to get used to the idea, however.

"Well, what else am I supposed to do?" she yelled back. "You won't let me help you! You treat me like some kind of stranger ever since Mom died. Why, Dad? Why are you acting like this?"

She was always blaming me for things, never taking responsibility for her own actions. It was infuriating. This was where I usually handed over control, allowed myself to be handled, worried about how my actions might affect *her*. Worried about the BAD of things. You know, like a GOOD parent is supposed to feel. But I thought again about the puppet prophet.

I grabbed the strings and pulled with all my might.

"Because I don't love you. I never loved you. You never brought me any joy."

She looked like I slapped her. She immediately started sobbing, and covered her face with her hands. To my surprise, I didn't feel sorry at all. In fact I felt as GOOD as GOOD can get.

When she finally calmed down she looked at me, her face twisted into an expression I have no name for, even now.

"Fine. You don't love me. Well, I don't love you. You're a horrible old man and you won't have to worry about me coming here anymore!" She got up from the sofa and marched to the front door, stopping only for a second after opening it.

"You didn't deserve my mother."

I think she thought that might hurt me, that it might make me feel as BAD as she did. She was wrong.

"She never brought me joy either. I'd have been better off without her."

Her face a mask of pure fury, she slammed the door, stood wailing on the front porch for a bit before leaving.

Good riddance, I thought, feeling alive for the first time.

I went back to my breakfast, which had gotten cold.

It tasted great.

As I was placing my dirty plate into the sink I heard organ music coming from the front room.

I made it to my chair just in time to catch the words *The Abattoir Hour of Truth* scroll across the screen in big, blocky red letters, before the picture changed to that of an inordinately obese man wearing an ill-fitting white tuxedo and no shoes sprawled out in a ratty old recliner, itself spotlighted and setting in the center of a darkened room. In his left hand—which rested languidly over the arm of the chair—he clutched a thin black book. His right hand waved at the air around his face.

Short, greasy hair pressed tight against the top of his too-large head, and his tiny eyes reflected back from behind amber-lensed glasses. He smiled, his teeth flashing an incongruent white, and leaned forward as the camera pushed in on his face, which had skin stretched across it that was much too smooth. His lips looked painted on.

He spoke.

"Brothers and sisters, I'm not here today to talk to you about sin or salvation. I'm here today to talk to you about truth. The gospel, if you will. But not the type of gospel you might expect from a man like me. No, brothers and sisters, I'm here today to talk to you about what is real. What *is* and what *is not*.

"Let me ask you something. How often in your life have you felt unseen? I mean really unseen. Not like when someone walks by you on the street without looking, or ignores you when you speak. I mean how many times have you felt like no one can see the real you, the true you? How many times have you felt like you are peeking through the bars of an iron cage, bars so close together only a slice of yourself can ever be seen at any given time? Brothers and sisters, I'm willing to bet that if you were to be truly honest the answer to that question would be: "Every day. Every moment. Always."

"I'm here to tell you why that is, and what you can do about it. I'm here to tell you that all you have to do is listen, and accept this gospel into your hearts. And the truth, if you'll pardon the cliche, shall set you free!

"I'll start with the bad news, just to get it out of the way. No one *can* ever really see you, or know you. It is impossible. There are simply not enough hours in a lifetime for you to give anyone a full understanding of the complexities of you. The picture they have will always be blurred and distorted by their own misconceptions, assumptions, and misinformation. This is inevitable, and you must accept this tragic fact. No one will ever see you, I'm sorry to say. Because there is no *you* to see."

He pointed right at the screen and stared, pausing for an uncomfortably long time before turning his head and continuing.

"But do not despair, brothers and sisters. Do not despair. Like I said, I started with the bad news.

"The *good* news is that you can change it. Yes you can. All you need to know comes from this good work right here." He held up the small black book and shook it back and forth. "This gospel tells us about the true nature of the universe, and of our place within it. It tells us that everything, including ourselves is, ultimately, nebulous; without true form or function. We are nebulous. Say it with me now. We are *nebulous.*"

The man stopped speaking again and looked directly out of the screen just as before. Squirming in my chair I eventually said, "We are nebulous," if for no other reason than to see what would happen.

He stretched his mouth wide and continued.

"Good. Now, what that means is that reality is what we make of it. You've no doubt heard the expression, 'A picture is worth a thousand words' or, 'Actions speak louder than words.' Well, brothers and sisters, turns out these are not merely contrivances, but statements of incontrovertible fact. And in order to give anyone a clearer picture of you, to make them understand, to feel a little more free of the cage that hides you, you must *act.* Show yourself to them. Liberate yourself through truth in action. Like this good book says, you must *grow before them.*

"And what does it mean to grow? I'll show you."

The man got up, his suit ripping in several places, and the light in the room began to intensify. The camera pulled away from him and eventually the walls and floors of the room could be made out.

They first appeared to be completely brown, splotched with white, but as the lights in the room got brighter I could just make out the fact that stuck to the walls and floor were every manner of small pest you could think of. Thousands of rats, roaches, ants, mice, weevils, locusts, and the like, had turned the interior of the room into a twitching canvas of death.

"Everything is stuck in place, fighting for its small piece of the universe, even you and I. But the difference is," the man started walking around the room, a disgusting, crunchy squishing sound following him, "because I have grown, I am freer than these smaller, less significant things.

"Right now you are bound by both your own idea of yourself as well as by the expectations and untrue beliefs of who you are, held by others. But remember, brothers and sisters, you are nothing and no one. You are nebulous—ever changing, without a true self. You can determine, from moment to moment, what your truth is. You can *act* and reform, and *grow* into anything.

"So do it."

The man then sat back down in the recliner, picking pieces of dead pests out from between his dirty toes.

The screen went black once again.

I sat back. It all made sense now.

I could feel the beginnings of a blurring at my edges.

I would act.

I knew what to do.

When Earl came by the next morning, I was ready. He fumbled through the back door, actually announcing himself for once. "Carl? It's Earl. You home?" He was probably confused by the darkened house, as I had turned off the lights save for the ones in my living room in order to lure him.

As he stood inside my kitchen doorway and looked out into my front hall I folded myself out of the pantry and crept up behind him, crouching on the balls of my bare feet. He never heard me coming.

Stretching, I grabbed him around the mouth and thrust my hunting knife up through the base of his skull. I gave it a twist and he collapsed into me, almost knocking me over. My old knees roared as I eased him to the floor. I pulled out the blade and wiped it on his trousers.

Sitting down at the table, I plucked a fresh cigarette out of the crumpled, old pack I'd retrieved from behind the furnace, one I'd stowed away after I had been forced by my daughter to hide my habit before I'd finally quit. It tasted GOOD, despite its staleness.

Earl's eyes were open and staring at me. I vibrated as I gazed into them. I could feel myself changing, reforming.

I really was *nebulous*.

I wish Earl could have seen the smile on my face. I wish he could have seen how ridiculous he looked, staring up at me like a landed fish, mouth stupidly agape. I wish he could have seen me *grow*.

I mashed my smoke out into the saucer I was using as a makeshift ashtray, then got up and went back to the pantry, where I gathered the rest of the supplies I'd readied for this moment: several towels, a handful of garbage bags, and a handsaw.

I got to work.

After I dragged Earl into the living room and onto the tarp I'd positioned in front of the fireplace, the television came to life once again. I wasn't surprised at all.

On the screen this time was the man with the television head himself, standing stock still in the center of the black room, his head full of static.

As I prepared Earl for display, the man with the television head inched closer and closer until his head-screen completely consumed the display of the set he had left me. The static of his face grew louder and louder, then settled into a low whine.

When my presentation was complete, I sat down in my recliner and lit another of my musty smokes.

The screen changed one last time.

It reflected me, nude and covered in blood, surrounded by yellow smoke, the bright cherry of my cigarette lighting a face that no longer resembled the one I used to think of as my own. I gripped the butt end between my teeth and gave a smile. My mouth stretched unbelievably wide. I laughed out loud and the cigarette tumbled down onto the floor, landing in a splash of sparks. The air filled with the smell of burnt carpet.

I kept on laughing.

I'm still laughing now.

Soon Karen will be here because Earl hasn't called to report in. She'll see what's become of him, what I've done, and she'll scream. She'll look and she'll finally see me for what I always could have been if not for her and her exhausting finger of a mother.

Then, I'll show her just how far I'm willing to go to be free of her.

I will grow before her eyes.

And it will feel GOOD.

Timmy Thomerson's Turn

As they made their way to the usual spot, all of the K-Mart Specials were thinking precisely the same thing: The Halloween of '86 *was going to be legendary!*

The group was decked out in fancy new costumes for the new year and was eager to show them off. Be it Cassie Peterson's Rainbow Brite, Johnny Saxon's He-Man, Richie Miller's Megatron, or Jeff Combs's ALF, this new cast of characters were all top-shelf, as far as the Specials were concerned, and infinitely better than the discount stuff they were usually forced to go out in.

They were giddy at the night's prospects not just because of their fancy new duds, but also because the chosen field of battle was to be very different from years previous. Johnny had decided that this year, instead of trolling the dregs of their own impoverished neighborhood, they would instead make their way over to the new housing development that had gone up in the last year, the one with all the big fancy houses that looked alike. The one that pushed out little rich turds to torment them with oh-so-clever nicknames like "The K-Mart Specials."

"I bet those jerks in Shermer Oaks give out full-sized candy bars to those preppy little shits, so we're gonna get us some too," Johnny had said, and none of the Specials had said boo. After all, who didn't prefer full size to fun size? What's so fun about small? Nothing, that's what. No fun, just cheap—and they were all tired of cheap.

Being poor always sucked, but when you wanted to be Lion-O and all your parents could afford was a homemade hobo or a discount devil, Halloween could be especially harrowing. But this year was different. This year they'd shot for the moon on the back of their parents' worry and guilt, and because Johnny's mom was a teacher, he'd said it had been a blessing in disguise when they'd all had to watch that poor lady teacher explode into space. He'd leaned hard all year on that tragedy, and when costume time came, he finally found He-Man an attainable goal.

Of course, the rest of the Specials followed his lead. They always did. Johnny rarely steered them wrong, and since it turned out he was right about the costumes, he must be right about Shermer Oaks too. Visions of giant Chunkys and Mr. Goodbars danced in their heads. Yippee!

So excited at the prospect were they, that no one even brought up Timmy Thomerson, except for when Johnny had said that since Timmy couldn't take his turn, *he* was next in line to pick the yearly route. Because the Specials didn't like to talk about Timmy, no protest was made on his behalf. Timmy wouldn't have minded, they thought. Timmy had loved trick-or-treating with them and had worn his trusty poverty-sheet each year with pride—pastel flowers and all—no matter how much Johnny had made fun of him for it. He'd have wanted them to have a good time.

As the group converged at the corner of Dekker and Henenlotter, they found the intersection surprisingly empty, hardly a fellow candy grubber in sight, except for one little kid who stood under the streetlamp wearing an eerily familiar flowery sheet with holes cut out for eyes.

It looked like Timmy had made it after all. But that was impossible...even on Halloween.

It was impossible because, two months prior, during the hottest July on record, Timmy had gone missing on the same day the other Specials had ditched him in a Safeway parking lot. Afraid he might tell on them for drinking ill-gotten beer in the woods behind the high school, they'd told Timmy they would meet him by the cart corral near the store's entrance. That way, they figured, when some enterprising adult finally noticed him lingering, his mother would be called to come get him and take him home. But Timmy never made it home that day. He was found two weeks later floating facedown in the reservoir wearing nothing but soiled socks, shoes, and underwear.

Dead.

Murdered.

What else had been done to him though, their parents wouldn't say. The subject became forbidden in their houses, even after the cops caught the guy in September trying to lure Babs Crampton into his van. When a kid at school said he'd heard his parents use the word "mutilated" when referring to Timmy, Johnny had socked him upside the head but good. Timmy's death had been a sore spot for Johnny especially, since they were cousins. His aunt still wouldn't come to visit his house if he was there. Seeing what couldn't have been Timmy now standing in their meeting place was akin to the highest of insults to Johnny.

Johnny got hot. He snatched his plastic mask off forcefully, handed it to Richie. He marched right up to the little kid and towered over him menacingly, practically on his tiptoes. The others followed just behind, stopping a few feet away.

"What're you doin' here, kid? You tryin' to catch a beatin'?" asked Johnny. "I don't know who put you up to this, shithead, but they didn't do you any favors sending you out here to mess with us." Johnny cracked his knuckles into his palm suggestively, like an action-movie tough guy.

The figure remained unmoved by Johnny's display.

It's my turn.

The words came from the ether, whispering into their brains like an invasive thought, and had the quality of something played on an old radio; a recording of someone talking from inside a deep hole.

No, not just any someone, thought Jeff.

The faraway voice in their heads was Timmy Thomerson himself.

Johnny did his best to maintain his tough demeanor, but Jeff heard the crackling of his vinyl costume rustling against his Wranglers. Johnny backed up a step, slowly turning to the group, his candy bag shaking in his hand. He-Man was afraid. The Power of Grayskull had failed him. Johnny's mouth moved up and down cartoonishly, like something out of a black-and-white comedy show they showed on *Nick at Nite*.

Cassie stepped forward. "Timmy? Is that you?" she asked, voice quivering as she reached down to grip the bottom of the sheet, the edge of which was ringed with a dark stain that dripped but didn't pool.

Her hand passed right through the fabric, which wobbled impossibly like a disturbed pond reflection. She gasped and jumped away, nearly knocking Richie to the ground. He caught her with both arms, and she let him hold her for a moment before pushing him away.

"Get off me, weirdo," she said, smacking him on the arm.

Richie was too scared to respond.

Jeff was scared too, but decided to take control, since Johnny was clearly at a loss.

"Hey, Timmy, how...um...how are you... I mean, uh...what are you, um... What's up?"

It's my turn.

It all proved too much for Johnny to take. Wild-eyed, he threw his arms into the air.

"I don't have to put up with this," he said, looking to each of the other Specials in turn, frantically searching for an ally.

He found them each too terrified to be of any use.

"This is some kind of stupid joke," he said finally, before turning and marching toward Hooper Drive, at the end of which a hole in a chain-link fence awaited. "I'm going to Shermer Oaks. You all can come if you want."

Johnny didn't make it ten feet before he stopped dead in his tracks and stood stiffly in the middle of the street. His body rose several inches into the air. His limbs were violently thrust out in four opposite and extreme directions. He floated there, suspended for several moments, and the rest of the Specials could do nothing but look on in awe. Slowly, his head and limbs began to twist about, and they saw stark terror on his contorted, frozen face. His eyes ran with unchecked tears, and the screams splitting his mind apart could just be glimpsed, crackling behind his wide pupils. His twisted mouth twitched with the wanting to unleash them.

The Specials held their breath. For a few brief seconds, all sound ceased to exist as each of them stared into the eyes of their leader, tormentor, brother, and friend. They watched him shriek silently while his head and arms and legs all reached their breaking points.

Finally, the air was split by five sharp cracks that traveled down their spines like cold fire. Johnny sagged and pirouetted as the ghost of Timmy Thomerson moved to stand beside him. Johnny jangled and jostled about, as if suspended from invisible strings, and the Specials gaped in horror at the spectacle before them.

Let's go, said Timmy, again inside their heads.

No one objected.

They made their way up Henenlotter Lane coming out onto the more populated Quigley Street, where Timmy and his family used to live (his mother and father having now moved away). Timmy and Johnny walked ahead, although Johnny mostly dragged his feet as he waggled along on Timmy's left.

Cassie, Richie, and Jeff lagged behind, but not too far, afraid of what might happen if Timmy thought them uncooperative.

Up and down Quigley Street they went, then Campbell followed by Cunningham, Carpenter, and Winston, following the exact plan Timmy had laid out in the crayon map he'd provided to each of them the week before his disappearance. Jeff still kept his copy on his nightstand.

By the time they'd finished, they all had bulging sacks that dragged the ground, even Johnny—whose bag now, presumably, belonged to Timmy. Not one of the adults noticed the ghastly way Johnny's neck and limbs lolled about at absurd angles. They all carried on as if nothing was amiss.

"I love your costume!"

"What are you supposed to be?"

"You're that cat eating puppet! My kids love that show!"

The same banal platitudes they heard every year, as if their friend's head wasn't on backward.

Jeff somehow knew it was Timmy's doing. He wasn't letting them see.

Once they'd made their way back to where they'd started, under the sickly light of the Dekker Avenue streetlamp, the Specials were relieved. The night was over, Timmy had gotten to take his turn, and there had been no more ugly incidents. Too bad about Johnny though, but leaving Timmy stranded in the Safeway parking lot had been Johnny's idea in the first place. And it had been Johnny's idea not to tell. Maybe

Halloween had finally loved Timmy back and made sure he'd gotten his stolen turn. Maybe it had punished Johnny for stealing it.

The haul was nice, even for the poor side of town, and while comparing their respective treasure troves, they momentarily forgot about the ghost and his grisly marionette floating only a few feet away.

They chatted nervously until they realized it was getting late, and Timmy was still watching.

Cassie was the first to try and say goodbye.

"Okay, Timmy, well, it was nice to see you, but I think it's time I got home. My mom's probably worried sick and well, I just don't want to get into trouble, y'know? So, I'll see ya later, and I hope you enjoyed trick-or-treating." She turned to walk away, glancing nervously at her friends.

Timmy's ghost merely shook its head, and their bulging sacks deflated as the goodies inside disappeared. The air went wrong. The Specials all became dizzy and wobbled in place. Cassie stood aghast, staring at the sky above her as she saw the stars reorder themselves, returning to a previous arrangement.

It's my turn.

Shaking, blinking in disbelief at each other and the empty pillowcases they clutched, the Specials dropped their heads and dutifully followed the apparition and its puppet, who were already making their way back up Henenlotter Lane.

The fourth time through, Jeff noticed that no one could really see their group. The crowd just parted magically for them on the sidewalks and streets, on the front walks and porches.

By the sixth time, the adults were only complimenting Timmy's costume, something they had almost never done when he was alive.

On the ninth, there were hardly any other kids at all.

After the twelfth, Cassie had had enough.

"I won't go again," she cried, throwing her candy sack to the ground and ripping off her Rainbow Brite mask. "I can't do it. My legs hurt. I'm hungry. I'm tired. I want to go home."

She glowered at Timmy's ghost and stomped both of her feet emphatically, placing balled fists on her hips, elbows akimbo—a familiar type of tantrum for her.

Timmy's ghost merely stared, its vacuous black eye holes stretching and leaking down its front, then snapping back into place to do it over again. It waited placidly for Cassie to finish.

"I am DONE!" Cassie screeched. "You can't do this to us. We didn't do anything wrong. It wasn't our faul—"

Cassie *was* done. Her angry words were reduced to a whimper that died before it reached the back of her teeth. Her eyes bugged alarmingly. Her lips pressed themselves together hard, stifling whatever was pushing out her rounding cheeks. She clawed at her neck and face, her mouth, leaving jagged marks with the naturally long nails her mother had insisted she grow if she wanted to wear polish. Her throat bulged grotesquely. She fell to the ground, writhing and kicking the air as she suffocated on the unspent bellows now exploding her throat. After some time, she gave one final convulsion and then went still, the sack of flesh beneath her chin coming to rest upon her upper chest, deflated, much like the candy bags. When she rose to take her place beside Timmy and Johnny, she resembled a dead-eyed frog from Rainbow Land.

Richie let out a long, ear-piercing wail that transformed into a fit of coughing.

Timmy allowed him to finish and gather himself.

Let's go.

For the next three trips, Richie was inconsolable. His movements were listless, and he sporadically sobbed, slowing dangerously on more than one occasion, so much so that Jeff was forced to physically hold him up and pull him along.

By the sixteenth, however, he'd settled himself into a scraping, zombie-like march, becoming another dead-eyed participant in the gruesome procession.

Jeff found himself valiantly attempting to hold back the advance of a new horror growing in the pit of his stomach. He continually fought the urge to glance at the sky, for the stars had disappeared, leaving only a vast, black Void.

He also ignored the warped expressions on the faces of the adults who now robotically provided only Timmy's favorite treats. Their comments and praises to Timmy became increasingly nonsensical with each new tour, and Jeff learned to avert his gaze away from their spasming eyes as these oddments spilled from their mouths. He was sure that to do otherwise was to invite madness.

"I bet a little ghost like you deserved to have a dog."

"That costume looks a lot better than what you were wrapped in, I reckon."

"The blade moved slowly, but the skin pulled quick. You took it like a champ!"

"The hole sounds different from inside, huh, Tim?"

"Remember, the Black Goat eats what it wants, it's young to dine eternally."

"For you, little Timmy, nihility will wait."

By the twenty-fifth, the cycle was solidly set, and just as Jeff thought he might be getting used to the insanity, Timmy changed up the routine.

Up to that point, they had not visited any of their own houses, as their parents never stayed home on Halloween. There were just too many bars and parties to go to with the kids away. Too much expensive candy to not have to buy or give out. For this reason, the remaining two Specials found that twenty-sixth trip incredibly jarring.

Upon exiting Henenlotter on that trip, they saw that the first stop was not to be Mr. Holland's redbrick bungalow on the corner of Quigley Street. Instead, in its place, right where it shouldn't have been, Richie's house loomed.

There was light pouring out of the windows and a car in the driveway. Someone was most certainly at home. Jeff tried to put his arm preemptively under his friend for support, but it didn't matter. As far down the block as they could see, on both sides, every house was the same—the same rusty car in the driveway, the same windows alight.

It was finally enough. Richie broke.

He tore off his mask and screamed into his palms. He wept uncontrollably, before lowering his hands and casting a manic, pitiful look at Timmy's ghost, which had turned to watch.

"C'mon, Timmy, please. It wasn't our fault. You know me and Jeff always tried to look out for you. At least let *us* go. We didn't know what was gonna happen when we ditched you. How were we supposed to know you'd get snatched? You were always hangin' around, whinin' about wantin' to do this and that. Everything had to be your way. Sometimes we just wanted to do older-kid stuff. You know? We didn't mean for what happened to happen. We didn't know what that psycho would do to you. Please, PLEASE, let us go! We're sorry, okay? We're SORRY!"

Time stood still, with no sound to be heard except for Richie's ragged snuffles.

Then, Richie's breathing hitched, and both boys found that they could no longer move, their gazes forcefully trained on Timmy. The terror in their eyes practically bled into the night, for Timmy's sheet was slowly rising up in the front, revealing the horror beneath.

He was naked except for his shoes and socks and Smurf Showtoon underwear. His body was crisscrossed all over with deep gashes that oozed and dripped, the droplets that came from them falling and returning, glitchy, like a VHS recording being rewound over and over. The skin of his face was gone, an irregular line of flesh ringing the place where it should have been, and his broken jaw gave his yawning, toothless mouth an unhinged quality. His skinless chin moved in the same schismatic way of his seeping blood.

Both boys wet themselves.

A new voice slithered into their thoughts, wet and phlegmy.

Hey, kid, you lookin' for your friends? Hop in, I'll take you to 'em. They told me I could find you here.

No one's coming for you, kid. No one can hear you. You can stop all that screaming.

You gotta stay real still now, or the knife's gonna slip and take off more. Okay?

Your pain will nourish the Thousand Young.

Then, it was Richie's voice inside their heads, only with the same distant quality of Timmy's, like a memory broadcast over the air.

You're like our little brother, kid. Our little brother, kid. Little brother, kid. Little brother. Brother.

The words faded out, echoing into oblivion, and Jeff saw the same look come over Richie that had come over Johnny and Cassie.

A thin, red line materialized and wrapped around his face, and innumerable lacerations appeared on the backs of his hands. He looked at Jeff with an almost perverse beseechment, but Jeff turned away just in time to miss the rest. But, even with his hands over his ears, he still heard the ghastly ripping sound that turned his stomach over like a car engine. He heaved, and a thin line of bile dribbled out of his ALF mouth and down his chin. He didn't dare take off his mask.

When he had the nerve to look up, he saw that Timmy's sheet was down and his melting black eye holes were on him.

It's my turn, said Timmy's ghost.

"I know, Timmy, I know it's your turn," said Jeff, picking up his empty sack and taking his place in the ghoulish procession, beside the bloody-faced Decepticon leader that used to be Richie.

Let's go.

"Yeah," said Jeff, sighing deeply. "Let's go."

The Face Dealer

That Bronson was ugly there was never any doubt. As far back as he could remember he'd been told it, and had never been allowed to forget. His striking ugliness was such that he had almost no memory of another's visage not twisted by revulsion. He'd become accustomed to it. His world was ugly and he was ugly and this was just the way of things. But then, there came Belinda.

Fair and merciful was the face that ducked into the blacksmith's stall that day, and the woman it belonged to beamed over him a smile with no twitch, one that fully enveloped eyes that did not squint or look away. She spoke with a summery voice and graced him with the rarified treasure of pleasant conversation. His ears and heart filled with ambrosia, he reshod her chestnut mare, glad of the sweat that streaked his soot-stained cheeks and masked his runnelling tears. He loved her deeply and immediately. How could he have not?

It was this love that sent him to Murvelo, a rapscallion of the highest order. Not even an angel such as her could love a man like him, not with these features, and Murvelo was known to truck with things normally steered right clear of. Bronson was sure he would have a solution, or at least would know where one could be found.

He was also sure Murvelo would, no doubt, charge much for the information, but for Bronson money was no object. He was a man in love and as skilled in smithing as he was ugly. No one cared if a smith was hideous as long as he did good work, and Bronson's work was always immaculate.

Murvelo haggled, then sold him a name and a map for separate, exorbitant prices. Both led Bronson to a crumbling tower deep within the woods, where the graying old sorcerer who lived there sat listening intently to his story wearing a bemused expression.

"Murvelo, eh?" smirked the sorcerer. "And just what name did he sell you?"

"He called you 'The Face Dealer,'" said Bronson, keeping his eyes low.

"And so I am," said the sorcerer, rising from an ornate chair and rounding his desk to stand before Bronson. He lifted the smith's chin delicately with two fingers and looked deeply into his eyes.

"I need you to understand a few things before any deal can be made between us. First, this will hurt. There will be more pain than you can imagine. Second, there is no turning back. Once the deal is made it cannot be undone. Do you understand?"

Bronson gave a firm nod. "I do."

"I need you to think very hard now. Ugliness such as yours is more unique than the hum-drum handsomeness you seek. A handsome man may be uncommon, but something this beastly is scarcely encountered, even by myself. It could be considered a gift, given the proper perspective."

Bronson scoffed and fixed the sorcerer with a look of grim doubt.

The sorcerer continued.

"I also want you to consider that this young lady may not care that you are ugly. She may enjoy you simply for you. She could be gifted with rare virtue, you know? You may not give her enough credit."

Bronson scoffed again. "I am not taken by such fancy. She is indeed extraordinary, to be sure, but there is no love in her eyes when she looks at me, only the same gentle kindness she has for all her fellow man. I would have more."

"Very well," said the sorcerer, moving back behind the desk. Reaching into one of its drawers he retrieved a piece of parchment and pushed it across to Bronson. "Review this document carefully before you sign."

Because of his looks, Bronson had never been properly schooled. He could not read, but could hide this disability well. He scanned the document carefully, moving his eyes side to side in even strokes, pretending. After an appropriate amount of time, he pushed the paper back across the desk to the sorcerer, who again looked bemused.

"Everything appears to be in order."

The sorcerer reached for Bronson with both hands.

"Give me your wrist," he said.

Bronson complied.

The sorcerer produced a small knife from his pocket and brought it swiftly across Bronson's palm. Bronson winced. The sorcerer then plucked a fresh quill from the desk and dipped it into the pooling blood. He clapped it firmly into Bronson's uninjured hand.

"Make your mark," he said.

Sheepishly, Bronson signed the bottom of the document with a large, ragged *X*. Taking the parchment from him, the sorcerer rolled it up and stowed it away.

"Let's get started then," he said, rising once again from his chair.

Bronson was led to an antechamber filled with pungent smoke. The sorcerer's apprentices lashed him to a chair while the sorcerer began to chant an archaic refrain.

Indeed there was pain. Typhonic gales of agony produced waves that crashed against his body, eroding his sanity infinitely faster than any cliff succumbed to the sea. Kept conscious by a myriad of philters and elixirs, he thrashed under his restraints. He gnashed his teeth at the sorcerer's odd apprentices as they applied caustic unguents to the totality of his newly shaven head. They jammed the burning ointments into his mouth and nostrils and he choked as he begged. His nose and throat were filled with the acrid tang of bubbling immolation. The apprentices were unmoved beneath their dark hoods, behind their blank porcelain masks. Their Void-like eyes of pitch remained unmerciful as they silently slathered, unnaturally calm.

Afterward, the sorcerer approached and oh-so-carefully peeled off Bronson's face. With this, consciousness slipped, despite the drugs' embrace.

When Bronson came to he was still restrained, but was no longer in the antechamber where his torture had taken place. Instead, he sat in a dining hall at the head of a large oaken table, which stood empty save for a row of candles and a single place setting filled with food, situated at the opposite end. Behind this place setting sat the sorcerer wearing Bronson's newly flayed skin.

Bronson tried to form words, but his mouth was lined in seared flesh. He widened his burnt-out eyes and wondered how it was that he could see. His breathing quickened as he drew it through scorched slits. His gasps were as raging hells. Had he the ability, he would have wept from sheer madness. The sorcerer laughed and waved a hand above his head.

A cadre of the unnerving assistants filed into the room and seated themselves in rows on either side of the table. They turned to Bronson and stared with vacuous, black gazes from behind their blank-planed facades. Slowly, they let down their hoods revealing bald, scarified heads to match his own. They removed their masks.

Their faces were horrific in their blankness. There were no eyes, no lips, no noses, only fissures, black holes of nothingness that howled softly as they breathed. Bronson attempted to scream but could manage only a jagged, trembling wheeze. His chin moved in silent moaning as his head lolled in horror.

The sorcerer massaged his stolen face, Bronson's face, and looked across to him with his own eyes. His smile was abhorrent.

"You should never trust a man like Murvelo, or one such as I, for that matter. You should have trusted the girl. I suspect she understands how wonderful this uniqueness truly is. There is nothing like it in my collection. Quite beautiful in its own way. I offer to you my genuine gratitude."

The sound of the sorcerer's voice coming from his mouth set Bronson shivering.

"I believe Murvelo did try to warn you, however, for he afforded you the true name of my occupation. Tragically, you misheard it. He liked you a bit I think, after all, if you had not come he would not have been paid. He will be paid for his treachery, however, I assure you. Perhaps you can take some comfort in that."

The sorcerer snapped his fingers and Bronson was grasped firmly from behind. As food was forked into Bronson's old mouth, into his new slit mouth was forced yet another foul-tasting intoxicant that set him instantly adrift in lethargy. The last thing he heard while still fully himself was wicked laughter pealing from his stolen face. The last thing he saw was a porcelain prison descend.

Belinda came by the blacksmith's stall every day the following week. She left disappointed each time.

The Last Case of Dr. Jonah Wexley Abbott

Steadily dripping onto the front porch of White Manor, Dr. Jonah Wexley Abbott found himself regretting many life choices. Squinting into the darkness past the porch's railing, he attempted to scan the length of the house, looking for movement within. Finding he could see nothing past the pustulant glob of gaslight cast by the lantern overhead, Jonah rubbed his temples and let out a frustrated sigh. He had a head full of cotton, a throat still soaked with the sour tang of old mash, and while the October rain had done much to sober him, could still feel the velvet pull of the whiskey behind his eyes. Shaking his head in an effort to beat back unconsciousness, he quietly recited a familiar affirmation of future clean living, and lifted his hand to knock again on the large front door.

Normally not considered an ungodly hour by most devout drinkers, this particular three-in-the-morning had found Jonah snoring away the effects of an early afternoon bout with the bottle. As always, Jonah had thrown the fight early, collapsing in a dingy heap on his office sofa, hoping not to be disturbed until tomorrow. When tomorrow came, however—heralded by the splitting sound of his ringing phone—he was completely unprepared for its arrival. As if ashamed of its intrusiveness, tomorrow brought with it several presents for him to open, and if his throbbing head, soggy clothes, and tired eyes were examples of its generosity, Jonah doubted he would enjoy any further unwrapping. He'd often found that tomorrows gave lousy gifts.

Shifting back and forth in his wet loafers, he took some pleasure in the disgusting sound they made, like churning, squashed bugs. Smiling in spite of himself, Jonah thought about what he would say to Gretchen once he saw her. Her audacity had been a problem before, but this latest stunt was unheard of. Having not received word from her for nearly half a year, Jonah had expected that when the occasion finally did come it would have at least been at a more reasonable time of day.

Before working himself up again, however, he resolved to err on the side of professionalism, and remain calm in the face of his grievances. After all, it was possible this early morning summons amounted to an *actual* emergency, and if it was of the type that required his expertise then he would assuredly need a cool head, no matter how much it was pounding. He did allow himself one final buffet on the door to vent any lingering hostility.

As if recoiling from his blows the door flew open, and a rush of torrid air hit Jonah squarely in the face. Inside, the foyer was distorted, like a reflection on the surface of a soap bubble. The wavy heat watered Jonah's eyes, causing him to flinch and blink furiously. Once his vision cleared, he was met by the stark form of White Manor's butler, Wilfred Holmes. Tall and lithe, Holmes was a serious man who normally reminded Jonah of a mortician or possibly a fallen priest. Now, however, his sallow, sagging skin and sunken eyes gave him more the look of a grizzled old dog.

"Good evening Dr. Abbott. I apologize again for the dreadful conditions and, of course, for your wait at the door," said Holmes, beckoning Jonah inside. "Please allow me to take your wet garments. I'll see to them and fetch you something warm and dry from the late Mr. White's bureau. I believe he was about your size."

The thought of wearing a dead man's clothes gave Jonah slight pause, but he was too tired and miserable to argue the point, and forcefully sloughed off his sodden outer layer with a grunt. Favoring Holmes with a half-hearted "thank you," he watched the butler hurry away before adjourning to the adjoining den.

Plopping down into one of the dusty, overstuffed armchairs in front of the fire, Jonah closed his eyes and leaned into the radiating heat. Flooding his nose with singed air, he gave a comfortable sigh. The echo of sleep's delicate dirge began again reverberating in the back of his mind. Snapping his eyes open, he searched the room for distraction. Above the fireplace he found it.

Striving to appear every bit the variety of New England upper crust expected of his family, Alastor White had been a collector of high society's most obvious relics. Never feeling like he had the respect of his peers, he opted instead to let the comforts of wealth abide his ego. The den was littered with evidence of his monetary vanity, but nothing captured the repulsiveness of his ostentation more than the painting cresting the mantle.

Most likely originating from the estate of some long-forgotten European lord, the piece was ill-sized for the space in which it had been placed. Gangling past the edges of the mantelpiece, the monstrosity seemed to hover over the room like a floating portal into a bizarre dreamscape.

Traditionally a more benign scene, this tableau of men and dogs hunting had always filled Jonah with dread. The men and their charges loomed like specters across a dark hill in the background, their eyes flashing like drawn steel, while the foreground was littered with terrified foxes tearing through the rushes. The sheer panic captured in the creatures' faces never failed to catch Jonah's breath in his throat. It was the wild-eyed look of the damned.

Utterly engrossed, he nearly leapt from his seat when Holmes's baritone sounded out, breaking his ensorcellment.

"Here you are, Dr. Abbott," said Holmes, handing him a plush robe and slippers, "I've brought fresh coffee as well."

Gracing the butler with a wan smile, Jonah slipped into the dry clothes and dutifully took the proffered cup and saucer. He waited for Holmes to sit down in the chair opposite before speaking.

"As much as I appreciate the hospitality, Holmes, I'd really like to know why I'm here, if you don't mind," said Jonah, sitting back down and taking a long pull of the rich coffee.

Easing himself onto the edge of his chair and leaning forward, Holmes fixed Jonah with a grave look.

"I can't really say, sir. After your students left, she instructed me to..."

"Wait," Jonah interrupted. "My students were here? Tonight?"

"Yes sir." Holmes's frown deepened. "I take it you didn't know."

"No, I didn't, but go on."

"As I was saying, she waited until they took their leave and then asked that I call you. I was to tell you only that the business was both urgent and work related, and nothing more. Not even that..." Holmes trailed off and his face became uncharacteristically distressed, turning a light shade of crimson.

"Not even what, Holmes?" Jonah straightened, his displeasure dissolving into curious anxiety. He'd known Holmes for over a decade and had never seen his stern decorum shaken so thoroughly, even when he'd sat in on meetings between Jonah and Gretchen that had devolved into screaming matches—or worse still, the ones that didn't. Even at those meetings when they'd spoken plainly of things others might only voice through whisper (or, better yet, not mention at all), the man's resolve had never wavered, yet now he seemed jolted to his core. It was enough to make Jonah shiver, despite the thick robe.

"Not even...that she is dying, Dr. Abbott. Not even that terrible fact," blurted Holmes, reaching into his breast pocket for a handkerchief.

"Dying?" said Jonah, mystified. "Of what?"

"Cancer, I'm afraid. She was first diagnosed about six months ago. It was shortly after that your students began coming to the house. I had assumed that you knew about her health and had sent them to assist her, that your lengthy absence was due to your search for a mystical cure of some kind. I didn't know until this evening that the widow had not informed you of her ailment. She didn't tell me. She said you didn't need to know before now. That you would only have 'gotten in the way,' whatever that means." Holmes dabbed his eyes.

"What *has* she been up to, I wonder," thought Jonah aloud, before standing and clapping the butler on the back. "Why don't we just go ask her ourselves? Shall we?"

Standing as well, Holmes replaced the handkerchief, cleared his throat, and straightened his waistcoat.

"Of course, sir. If you're ready, sir."

"Lead the way," said Jonah, waving his hand dramatically toward the doorway.

Following Holmes through the foyer and up the stairs, Jonah couldn't help but notice the state of disrepair the house had come under. Having crowned Whitecroft Hill since the time of the nation's independence, the house was certainly old, but had always been well maintained. Being one of the first American dynasties to wrest great wealth from the untamed woodlands of the north, the White family had always made sure to keep their grand estate in top form. They saw themselves as Massachusetts royalty, and anything short of stately simply would not do for their manor.

Royalty, however, requires a bloodline and this was something that Alastor and Gretchen found tragically unattainable. Being too proud to adopt, no heir existed to see to things and with Alastor in his late eighties at the time of his death, and Gretchen being nearly there herself, the upkeep of the estate had long ago fallen solely on Holmes and the rest of the help.

When most of the money dried up due to a combination of Alastor's bad investments and Gretchen's obsession with supernatural research, the help dried up as well. Holmes, even at a solid sixty-five, proved no match for the many daunting needs of the palatial beast.

He'd tried his best, at first, but eventually Holmes gave up the ghost and began focusing on making Gretchen as comfortable as he could in a small section of the house. The rest he surrendered to dilapidation. Jonah almost felt sorry for the willowy old hound before remembering that upon Gretchen's death the estate was to be liquidated with everything split evenly between Holmes and an endowment for the university. Even in its current state the house and the land it sat upon would be worth millions and would provide Holmes with more than enough reward for his dogged dedication.

Reaching the third floor, Jonah stared down the long hallway at the two enormous doors that led to the widow's chambers. As he moved toward them, his stomach tightened. His head swam and he imagined the doors as a giant maw, waiting to swallow anyone foolhardy enough to approach them. A feeling of uncertain doom washed over him, and being mixed with considerable weariness, caused him to lean heavily on the oak wainscoting just outside the bedroom.

"Are you all right, Dr. Abbott?" inquired Holmes, reaching out to him.

Swatting the butler's hand away wordlessly, Jonah took a moment to collect his frayed wits. Taking a deep breath, he steadied himself then turned to face the old man.

"Sorry. I just got a little overwhelmed. I'm all right now," he said, turning back to face the doors.

"Of course," said Holmes as he opened them, giving Jonah his first look at the dying Widow White.

She looked old. Not the type of old one earns at the end of a long and fruitful life, but old like rusted metal, blighted by rot. Her wasted arms, folded across her stomach with funereal grace, were sporadically stained by deep purple bruises. Propped up by two plush pillows, her shriveled head nestled in a shock of white straw hair. Under dark lids, her closed eyes floated in pools of shadow; fleshy orbs twitching at pained dreaming. Thin lips rattled her equally thin chest with struggled wheezes, filling the aseptic air with desperate gasps. It was almost more than Jonah could take.

Standing dumbstruck in the doorway, it took him several moments to find the legs beneath him. Upon finding them he attempted to move as quietly as possible to the bedside while dragging a chair over from the nearby vanity.

Sitting down, he leaned forward and stared at the widow for several moments, attempting to attune himself to this new reality. Absent-mindedly, he began stroking his mustache, a nervous habit he'd picked up in college while stressing over exams.

"I know you're sitting there stroking your whiskers at me. I could smell the liquor on your breath before you got to the top of the stairs," said the widow, startling Jonah upright and sending his hand quickly away from his face.

"I didn't want to wake you," said Jonah, turning away as Gretchen opened her eyes and tried to sit up in bed. Holmes rushed to her side but she smacked him away.

"Nonsense. I brought you here to talk about something important. I'd imagine I'd have to be awake for such a conversation, wouldn't you, *Professor?*" sneered the widow, condescension dripping from the corners of her mouth. Bristling, Jonah was reminded of who he was dealing with, illness or not. He proceeded accordingly.

"Okay then Gretchen. What *am* I here to talk about?"

"That's the spirit my boy! Now that we have that out of the way, I'll get right to it. Have you ever heard the name Augustus Rayburn?" The widow's milky eyes gleamed.

"As a matter of fact, yes I have. An acquaintance of mine mentioned this case to me a few months back. He thought I might be interested in looking into it. Rayburn was a ship's captain, brought back by his crew from an arctic voyage raving like a lunatic. They swore he'd made some kind of pact with a demon or some such nonsense after their ship had become lodged in ice. Claimed it had given him the knowledge to free the ship but had also driven him insane. Sound about right?" Jonah sat back, steepling his fingers arrogantly.

"Was that acquaintance Hunter Foley?"

"Yes... You haven't been dealing with that charlatan have you? I turned him away for a reason. He's a useless toad who does reckless, slipshod research and you should know better than to—" Jonah exclaimed, his face turning pink.

The widow interrupted.

"Calm down, you blowhard. I sought the man out myself, not the other way 'round. I was the one who told him about Rayburn in the first place. If he brought the story to you, I suspect he was merely trying to get you to do his work for him. I stumbled upon Rayburn's journal in one of the curiosity auctions I take part in. I only hired Hunter to authenticate it. What he found in that process is what I brought you here to discuss."

Jonah calmed himself, duly rebuked and intrigued. "What did he find, then?"

"Rayburn," said the widow, smiling. "Alive!"

"Ridiculous. Rayburn's been dead for over a century. I checked into it. He died in the fire that burned down the old asylum in Kingsport, where his family lived."

"Wrong. Rayburn was reported dead following the fire, this is true, but his body was never recovered. His family buried an empty coffin. I instructed Hunter to look to other crazy houses in the area, thinking that he might have wandered away during the confusion and gotten picked up by another hospital. I was only looking for records since none survived the Kingsport fire. At Danvers State Hospital, however, we found more than I ever could have hoped for.

"A janitor overheard the Danvers director give Hunter the run-around and pulled him aside as he was leaving the hospital. After considerable compensation, he told him about a patient that was kept in isolation that none of the staff would talk about. The rumor was that the patient had been in the hospital for decades with no family, not even a name. With a few well-placed phone calls to some of the hospital's most generous donors and several severe promises of discretion, I was able to get Hunter access.

"He took photos and made copies of the hospital's records. Suffice it to say, based on the evidence, we both believe that the madman he visited that day is indeed Augustus Rayburn, former captain of the Mary Margaret." The widow reached under her nightstand and dragged out a cardboard box. "And this should be all the proof you need."

Picking up the box, Jonah carefully removed the lid and looked inside. There was the journal, photos both new and seemingly ancient, and a stack of administrative folders full of yellowed, typewritten pages. Jonah laid it all out on the bed in front of him.

He started with the pictures. The oldest of them, dated some hundred years prior, was a studio-style portrait depicting a stern, dapper man alongside a young, ethereal woman in white. A wedding photo to be sure. Written on the back in rough strokes were the names "A. Rayburn" and "J. Rayburn." Second oldest was an intake photo from Danvers. Rayburn's face was slack, held still by a coarse hand erupting from hospital whites. He bore an unsettling, glassy stare that appeared fixated upon something well past the camera. Neither of these struck Jonah as particularly remarkable, but the most recent photos, taken only weeks prior, raised every hair on the back of Jonah's neck. It showed a man lying in repose inside a filthy padded room. Mired in the same grime that covered the walls, his face was difficult to decipher, but the eyes were exact. As if the intervening century did not exist, all the photos appeared to contain the same man, the same unchanged face. Remarkable.

The folders were next. The tale they told was one of greed, apathy and horror.

After being processed into the facility under the placeholder Richard Roe, Rayburn's initial few months were uneventful. His demeanor was peaceful and his behavior, while typical for a raving lunatic, was nothing too difficult to handle. He followed instructions, was never violent, and kept mostly to himself. His only vices seemed to be answering inquiries from staff and other patients in unsettling, riddlesome phrases, and standing perfectly still in the corners of rooms for hours on end. This all changed, however, following his first, and only, experience with a unique form of hydrotherapy.

The administrator of the procedure, a Dr. Ernst Melville, believed that exposing patients to near-freezing temperatures could shock their systems into a curative state, purging them of their toxic insanity. Melville had taken a particular interest in Rayburn, and became convinced that curing him was the key to validating his experimental treatment.

Wearing rubber diving suits lined with seal fat (of the doctor's own design), Melville and two nurses transported Rayburn to a remote bank of the Ipswich River at the peak of winter, and carried the near-nude man into the icy runnel, dunking him under. His reaction to this was both swift and savage. Bellowing incoherently, Rayburn burst from beneath the water, clawing and biting at the nurses that held him. When they let go in surprise, he turned his attention to the doctor. Melville lost an eye and most of his right hand before they could subdue the madman. A clean bite and prompt spit into the frozen froth were all that saved the physician's fingers.

Following this event, Rayburn was confined to a solitary room and labeled a "malcontent." He now ravened habitually, throwing himself against the walls of his cell day and night, repeating words and phrases that belonged to no known language. He attempted to attack anyone that interacted with him, and during one particularly violent exchange, fell awkwardly on his head, wrenching his neck grotesquely to one side. Hence, the discovery of his apparent immortality.

What followed was year upon year of ruthless experimentation done under abiding secrecy. At that time, as a ward of the state, Rayburn was at the mercy of his attendant professional, and Melville maintained a ghoulish grip upon him. Over the next two decades he was subjected to the terrible depths of the doctor's ever more depraved imaginings. Flayings, breakings, burnings, starvation, dehydration; in the name of science Melville twisted and tortured the former captain ceaselessly and recorded it all in chillingly clinical language.

Rayburn survived everything.

Eventually, this period of inhumanity ended, abruptly. An internal report alluded to an unfortunate incident during one of Rayburn's "intensive therapy sessions" with Dr. Melville. While no details were given as to the nature of this event, Rayburn was recategorized as "unstable" and moved to a remote wing of the hospital. At the recommendation of staff members, he was placed under constant restraint and only sparsely monitored. His records were sealed and classified as "Administration Only."

Hunter had affixed to the report a photocopy of an obituary

whose headline read **"Local Physician Laid to Rest."** A picture with the caption "Dr. E. Melville" was accompanied by a short, boilerplate article. The funeral was family only, and closed casket.

Afterward, there was nearly nothing. Since it was known that Rayburn needed neither food nor drink, none was provided. Since he took no sustenance, he produced no waste, so there was no need for him or his cell to be cleaned. From then on, his presence in the facility was only mentioned in the yearly audit where, for the purposes of state funding, he was counted, though few of the appropriated funds ever made their way into his care. He was left alone for the better part of a century in a padded tomb, a living monument to man's capacity for cruel indifference.

Disgusted, Jonah thrust the last folder into the box with a grunt and reached for the journal.

An ornate compass had been burned into the cracked cover, and the book was wrapped with a brittle, leather thong that held it loosely together. An ornamental anchor hung from the end of the binding, pendulous and vaguely foreboding. Delicately unwrapping the thing, Jonah was assailed by the acrid, musty scent of red rot. The rifled pages spewed the smell directly into his face and he sneezed loudly, much to Holmes's chagrin. The butler favored him with a grimace and a terse movement of his head, toward the widow. Jonah shrugged, then brought his attention back to the dusty tome.

Inside the front cover, inscribed with long-faded ink, were the words *from Josephine,* accompanied by a simple, delicate drawing of a flower. Jonah lingered on the words for a moment, running his thumb across them slowly before moving on.

The journal was nearly illegible. Age, improper care, and poor penmanship had conspired to ensure the record held onto its secrets. Luckily for Jonah, he'd spent a postgraduate year cataloging the antiquarian texts of Professor Karl Unkirch, whose poor pencraft was legendary, therefore the ancient seafarer's chicken scratch proved no challenge at all.

The book was primarily made up of entries from Rayburn's last journey, a foray into the frozen waters of the Northwest Passage, near Baffin Island. It was here that his ship was swallowed by the greedy ice that ruled the region. He and his men, hearty sea-dogs to the last, tried valiantly for over a week to free the craft, but freezing gales abutted the pack ice to create an insurmountable hyperborean blockade. When food supplies ran low and morale followed close behind, Rayburn became desperate. The ghosts of both the Erebus and the Terror haunted his dreams. The dread of joining with those ill-fated warships pushed him near to mania.

Serendipitously, at this critical time, the group was visited by a small delegation from an Inuit tribe who hailed from a nearby island. Speaking remarkably good English, they seemed eager to please and traded fairly with the men, so when they offered to help with their plight, Rayburn readily accepted. They claimed the ability to grant him the knowledge necessary to free his ship, but at great cost. When he assured them he would pay any price in exchange for the lives of his crew, the tribesmen agreed to take him, and him alone, to their village, insisting that the secrets they would reveal were for his eyes alone. Leaving his first mate in charge, Rayburn took all the gold he'd received in payment for the voyage and set out with the Inuit across the frozen sea.

Here, the journal was missing several pages. The torn, uneven remnants of those missing leaves were marred by dark, erratic marks left not by ink, but grease pencil, the use of which was sometimes favored by cartographers working under saturate conditions. Following this curiosity was a final log entry, left by First Mate Atticus Fields on the day before the Mary Margaret's homecoming, wherein he describes the events following Rayburn's return from his expedition.

Wrapped in thick fur, under which he was nude, their captain was spied in the early morning, some three days after venturing forth, alone and shuffling in the algid terrain some distance from the ship. Upon retrieval, he was found clutching his journal to his chest, which now contained several hastily drawn sketches intricately delineating the manner with which the ship could be extracted from the sea's wintry clutch. Although finely detailed, Fields noted how the alien schematics, along with their captain's near-catatonic state, inflamed the crew's standard, but substantial superstitions. Strange symbols of arcana supplemented the pictographic instructions along with one word scrawled again and again in the empty spaces: Xoathathum, the same and singular word Rayburn repeated ad nauseam throughout their excursion back to port.

After gaining their freedom, the crew burned the sinister scrawlings. Rayburn was locked in his cabin, and Atticus assumed command.

A glitter of recognition flashed annoyingly in Jonah's mind. Xoathathum. The word scratched at a cold, fearful place inside him. He placed the journal back into the box, his face the picture of perplexation. He then reached for his mustache again before catching himself. He opted instead to run a hand awkwardly through his unkempt hair. Looking up, he found Gretchen holding another old book in her hands. A wry smile scampered across her weathered features.

"Recognized that name too, didn't you? Well, I already took care of it. Here," she said, thrusting the folio at him. "Don't say I never gave you anything."

He was stunned. One of the few times in his life he'd been truly at a loss for words. She held in her hands the most seminal work of the warlock Ludwig Prinn. Carefully taking the volume from her, Jonah ran his hands over the shining black cover. With his finger, he traced the raised, gothic filigree and bold lettering emblazoned on its skin before reverently caressing the decorative, serpentine figure surmounting it all. Shuddering, he involuntarily breathed the name of the grimoire out loud.

"*De Vermis Mysteriis*," he said throatily. "Where did you get this?"

"I bought it, *obviously*. I'm rich, remember?" The widow chuckled, her wormy lips split by tiny, discolored teeth.

"This is the university's copy! These are Peaslee's notes in the margins. I can't believe they would sell it to you," said Jonah, thumbing quickly through the book.

"Well, they didn't exactly want to lose the endowment upon my imminent death so when I threatened to leave it to another university, they gave in. It's valuable but, as it turns out, not quite valuable enough to throw away millions."

"I bet," said Jonah drolly, recovering from his shock. Closing the book, he began unconsciously cradling it like a newborn baby. "Why would you go to such great lengths to acquire this?"

"You aren't that dimwitted, doctor, even when you've been awakened from a drunken stupor. Xoathathum is the reason, of course. I've already marked the page for you."

It then dawned on Jonah why the widow had summoned him. He threw the book onto the bed instinctively, shaking his head from side to side.

"Absolutely not, Gretchen. I won't do it. I understand what you're going through, but this is not the way!"

"YOU UNDERSTAND NOTHING," cried the widow, before breaking down into a caustic fit of coughing. Holmes, his face ugly with concern, hurried over and held a clean towel under her chin to catch the red, caliginous effluvia that rolled from her mouth. Regaining her composure, she continued. "Rayburn is still alive today. You've seen the proof. That doctor did everything he could to break that man and he survived it all. He doesn't age, for god's sake! I believe that those savages somehow knew how to conjure the creature for him. I believe it showed him how to free his ship. I also believe it gave him his eternity, something I need if I'm to continue on at all. Yet you would deny me *life*, after everything I've done for you? Are you that ungrateful?"

"It isn't a matter of gratitude, Gretchen. The man might have an eternity but his mind is broken. You would trade your sanity for life? What do you gain by becoming an immortal madwoman? These things are not to be trifled with. You don't know what you are asking!"

"Yes. Yes, it broke his mind, but he was an ignoramus. A simple ship's captain from over a century ago. Uneducated, unrefined. He and I are nothing alike," she said, tossing her head haughtily to one side.

"Regardless, I won't do it. I will not help you conjure your doom." Jonah rose from his chair and turned to address Holmes. "Now, if you would kindly retrieve my belongings I would very much like to return to my office and find whatever sleep I can before morning. Tomorrow, I will look for a more reasonable answer to your problem. Had you consulted me sooner, I might have been of more help than my students or that snake-oil salesman. I'll come by in the afternoon and we'll—"

Turning back to Gretchen, Jonah's words caught in his throat as he found himself staring down the barrel of a shining, pearl-handled revolver.

"Sit. Down," said the widow sharply, thrusting the gun at him with each word. "Now!"

Jonah sat, obediently.

"I thought you might give me a problem so I had Wilfred pull this old number out of mothballs in order to "persuade" you, should you refuse. I don't have the time or stomach to massage your ego or shout you down about this. I am standing at death's door and now, if you don't do exactly what I ask, so are you."

She waved the pistol dramatically.

"You gonna kill me?" he asked sarcastically, fear trickling down his spine.

"I'd encourage you to think very hard about what you know of me. Then, consider the situation I am in. I'm out of time, and you can help me find more. You can help me find it *all*. I've spent most of my life and nearly all of my husband's family fortune seeking the type of gift that simpleton Rayburn was given. *You've* caroused your way across half the world to try to find it for me. Do you think I would give up now because you are a coward? I told you when we started this endeavor of ours that I wouldn't stop until I got what I wanted. Well, here it is, sitting in front of you, so pick up that book and get to work, and ask yourself one last thing before you do. How serious do you think I am about staying alive?"

"Fine," said Jonah, reaching for the manual while shooting Holmes a quick, pleading look. The servant's face was stony and gray, and his baleful eyes betrayed no conflict. He clearly stood with his mistress on the issue. A thin frown paired with a clenched jaw were the only signs he held any guilt regarding his subterfuge. Jonah tried not to blame him.

The notated page was marked by a folded sheet of paper upon which was Hunter Foley's signature sloppy script. He had made a poor attempt to translate the ritual's invocation from an excerpt he had blasphemously highlighted in yellow. Jonah gritted his teeth. The man's manners appeared as uncouth as his Latin, for there were several key errors in his translation that stood out immediately. Jonah flipped the paper over and began his own transcription with a pen Holmes was quick to provide.

"You know this idiot didn't go to school, right?" he asked the widow, never taking his eyes from the task.

"Different dogs for different work, as my father used to say. Hunter has a nose for the unseemly and a willingness to roll around in it. He might not be the bloodhound you are, but he is a useful little mongrel who works for scraps. I only let him do that translation to placate him. He was so eager to please, it seemed wrong not to give him a pat on the head. Trust me, I knew which dog to call tonight. I know what you were bred for."

"Charming," said Jonah, favoring the widow with a withering glance. She responded with only a click of the tongue, and a tap of the gun's barrel to her palm.

After finishing the transcription, he spent the next half hour preparing the room with numerous candles, pungent incense, and profane, antediluvian markings. The butler and the pistol, spurred by the widow's barking orders, scrutinized his every move. Foley might have botched the translation of the ritual itself, but he was adept enough that Gretchen had a reasonable understanding of what was required for the preparation. She had also, apparently, had one of Jonah's brighter students check and correct Hunter's translated list of ingredients. He recognized the loopy, innocent longhand immediately.

He hated that they were involved. He had tried to keep them from his mistakes, to ensure that their curiosity remained strictly academic, never dipping into the practical. The practical was dangerous and coiling, lying in wait for fools to find it. Now they were as stricken as he, the promise of forbidden knowledge coursing through their minds. He hoped he'd live through this night if only to undo that harm, to walk them back from the brink he knew so well, prevent them from taking the same plunge.

After laying the groundwork, Jonah gave his translation a final once over. Upon this reflection, something significant occurred to him, something that could bring the entire insane enterprise to a halt. He moved slowly to the widow's side to show her. Holmes moved to the other, anticipating.

"Okay Gretchen, I don't want you to think I'm trying to trick you, but if you look here you'll see that Foley mistranslated this term. This is important because he told you that a "gift" was required but what it actually says is..."

He was silenced by two thunderous reports from the gun. Staggering back, he grabbed at the sides of his head, grasping for his ringing ears. Looking across the bed to Holmes, he saw the butler's eyes roll back as his hands spasmed wildly in front of him. Sagging forward, the wretched servant's head slopped gore out onto the coverlet before his body collapsed to the floor, all its strings cut.

"Sacrifice. You need a sacrifice. My Latin is better than Hunter's as well," said Gretchen coldly, pointing the pistol at him once again.

Jonah stared at the widow, blinking in disbelief before vomiting. Wiping his mouth, he moved to the end of the bed and, without hesitation, began the incantation, carefully avoiding a glance at Holmes's ruined visage.

It was a call to summon Xoathathum, the Worm of Midnight, and Keeper of the Key. Spawn of Havissik'Kri—the dreaded Serpent of Infinite Sands—Xoathathum and its progenitor were among several obscure beings worshiped by the various nomadic peoples who lent their knowledge to Prinn during his travels in Arabia. The two were considered creatures of great and powerful secrets, archivists of all the knowledge in creation. The ritual purported to summon the fiend who, upon being shown proper supplication, would bestow the gift of its vast wisdom upon the supplicant.

For several moments the recitation, rotely repeated, bore no fruit. The widow's displeasure was palpable though she was mindful not to disturb the recital. Slowly, however, the air in the room changed. The candles sputtered gravely. Jonah's voice dimmed in his ears as he was overcome by a rising cacophony of impossible sound. It thrummed and pressed from all sides. This phenomena appeared to emanate from the bedroom ceiling, which had begun warping in on itself, forming a growing hole of profane darkness. As it widened, a frigid blast erupted from the opening, sending him into a fit of involuntary shaking. Still, he pressed on. The widow was shouting something upward, a look of manic bliss splayed across her face. Jonah's ears were filled and he could not hear a thing above the eerie din that had suffused the air around him, but he could see joyous tears sliding down her face, pooling beneath her quivering chin. Finally, the hole reached a breadth that spanned half the ceiling. Then, all at once, the bedlam stopped. Then the beast came through.

It unfurled itself from the portal like a post-pupate insect and piled into a tremendous mass to the right of the bed. Resembling a giant segmented worm several dozen feet in length, Xoathathum's corpse-white flesh was pitted with small openings that gulped for air like drowning fish. The noise was odious and sickening. Its head was covered by two sightless, opalesque eyes that convulsed weirdly in their sockets. Maggot-like tendrils dripped from beneath the creature's open jaws, and the many rows of keen-edged teeth that filled its great maw seeped with a greenish ichor. Its underbelly was translucent and lined with hundreds of spindly, arthropodal legs that twitched and kicked and pawed. Just inside this diaphanous membrane thousands of smaller snaking figures swam about, slithering amongst one another furiously. The creature swayed in the air hypnotically and Jonah stared, dumbly silent until stirred by the crazed voice of Gretchen White.

"Oh mighty Xoathathum, Keeper of the Key, hear my plea," she screeched, beseeching the monster with outstretched hands, palms up in rogation. "Grant me the boon of your everlasting wisdom so that I may see the world through thine eyes, for all the years to come." She pointed at the corpse of her former servant.

"I offer this sacrifice as payment; a pittance offered in humility," she said, finishing her mottled version of the ritual's final plea, making sure Jonah didn't steal her treasure. Crafty old girl. Then, head bowed properly, she waited.

As crafty as she may have been, her Latin wasn't nearly as refined as she thought. Jonah grimaced as the beast's protuberate head slunk across the body of poor, unfortunate Holmes. It examined its gift closely. The slight sound of a thousand buggy leg parts scratching at the butler's remains gave Jonah a jellied feeling all over. A sharp, reedy howl rumbled out of each of its thousand tiny mouths as it pulled quickly up and away from the body, pupal whiskers buzzing. Unfortunately for her, Gretchen's gift was worse than any a tomorrow had ever given. Jonah knew that if there was one thing to know about this line of work it was this: Nothing can get you killed easier than arrogance coupled with inartful Latin. That, and offering a corpse to a god when live payment is due.

In less than a blink, it was on her; biting, grinding and swallowing. Burbled screams poured out and over its lower jaw along with gobs of bloody, ichorous sludge. Even after the screams died out, the sound of crunching and bubbling persisted. Jonah watched as the widow's gnarled feet twitched reflexively, hanging from the monster's mouth. He stupidly thought of a duckling kicking below the surface of a pond. A ghastly slurping sound rounded out the gruesome spectacle as the creature gave a final gulp and turned its attention to the good doctor.

Unable to move, Jonah watched as the thing squirmed across the floor with ropey spasms, closing the distance between them quickly. Rising up, its innumerable breathy apertures hummed an other-worldly tune. Beneath the surface of its gauzy belly, the nematodes were vibrating. They passed bright, colorful electrical pulses between them and a rainbow of carnival lights sparkled his eyes. The worm's chitinous appendages swam in concert with one another, swooping up and down like the paws of a begging terrier. Its tail became distended, and grew into a swollen bulb. The internal mass moved swiftly through the length of the beast, shimmering the prismatic grubs as it passed, shooting toward the toothy end. Heaving, the creature regurgitated, covering Jonah over with gory slime speckled with the remnants of his late employer. Clawing at his nose and mouth in an effort to breathe, he spat bits of bone and hair and bloody ooze onto the carpet. He could feel the substance soaking into his pores as his body alternated between sizzling and freezing. Trembling, he watched as Xoathathum appeared to give him one final consideration before burrowing back into the hole from whence it came, which closed behind it with a deafening thunderclap.

Falling to his knees, Jonah reached for the upended box on the floor beside the bed. He searched for and found the pen he'd used for his earlier transcribing, and attempted to scratch out as much as he could before the looming madness now growing in his mind consumed him. He could feel everything crackling in his head, gorging, pressing at the walls of his skull. He blinked against hallucinations begat by his senses being opened to the infinite. Believing himself creating a hasty account of his fated evening, he fluttered his eyes once more in the face of his mounting hysteria, and looked upon the pages between his white knuckles to see only thick depictions of it drawn in the manner of cavemen. These demented doodlings were surrounded by hoary, alien designs with the name of the god worm lain repeatedly between them.

Jonah flopped over onto the floor and cackled as he was pulled under, and submitted to the thrall.

His mind etherealized and he found himself awash in a sea of memories, each recalled with a clarity that made him mournful. Every familiar mistake pierced him as he traveled down thousands of previously covered roads, his newfound understanding only intensifying his remorse at all the terrible choices. He felt himself a mockery, an insignificant, crawling fruitlessly in cancerous muck. He could see the absurdity of human existence, the absolute joke his life had been. He moved beyond his birth and tumbled on a wave of time. Aimless and bobbing along, he eventually came to a nexus and gained purchase on vaguely familiar metaphysical ground.

An ending lay there, a precipice at the brink of a vast chasm of darkness that twinkled with an untold number of steely eyes, and warbled with the voice of eternity. Standing at this precipice, looking out into that rolling forever, impossibly, was Rayburn.

Jonah joined him.

Brought together by interpolated destiny, they each looked into the stygian depths and perceived their inescapable futures for the first time, dissimilar but the same. They saw their bleeding hands scrawling gibberish on the walls of the madhouse rooms to which they both would be committed. They saw the forlorn look in their loved ones' eyes as they thrashed and raved before them. They saw the barbarous experimentation they would endure, understanding that the immortal can still feel. They heard the discordant sounds of their endless keening, cries against pain, and indelible psychopathy. Finally, they saw the stricken faces of the ageless prisons that would carry their broken minds for eternity. Standing momentarily entwined in inexorable fate, they marveled as one at the immensity of their dooms.

Then, the ground gave way beneath them, and they both fell screaming into the Void.

THE YELLOW HOUSE

On the Night Bus

I am sitting at the bus stop. I am on my way home after work. The streetlight above me is dying. No, the streetlight above me is fluttering, not dying. It is important that I use better language.

This is day seventeen of the changeover and my assignment to nights. I am finally starting to feel comfortable about it. This is a roughly twenty-five percent improvement over my last shift change. I am encouraged by this. I feel like I can improve further, however, and I believe I will set my goal for the next changeover to an additional five to ten percent. It is important that I keep my expectations within reason. This will prepare me better for failure.

The fluttery light is making it difficult to write, and is giving me a vague sense of unease. I recognize this as the voice of fear. I must remember that I am no longer afraid of the dark. I am no longer afraid of being alone. It is okay that it is dark at night. It is okay that I am alone. I have purposely not used the word "always" before the word "alone" in the previous sentence. It is important that I be honest, but also try to stay positive about the future. As you have observed in the past, doctor, this journal should be a repository of honest thoughts, for that is the only way it can be of use to either of us. You are very wise.

That was not flattery.

I checked my watch. The bus is twenty minutes late. The voice of fear is starting to sound. I ignore it. Buses can be late for a number of reasons, not all of them sinister. There are many things that could be keeping the bus. It could have had to wait for a handicapped person or persons to board. It could have run out of gas. It could have a flat tire. It could have been in a wreck. The engine could have caught fire. All of these things are much more likely than the idea that the bus driver purposely missed my stop, or that a grand conspiracy has been hatched against me. This is the way the old me would see things. And I am new now.

It feels good to reject the voice of fear. I feel thankful the fluttery light and the late bus have given me the opportunity to do so.

It feels good to recognize this.

I hope the bus comes soon. It is very cold out.

The cold makes me nervous. Unfortunately, I have yet to master the art of silencing this particular sermon of fear. Tonight, I have only managed to get it down to a low whisper. This is an improvement, and I am glad of it, yet I do wish this whisper of cold were not with me right now, considering all the other factors at play. That is the truth.

The bus is coming now. It has a paper taped to the inside of the front window with its number printed on it in big block type. This is not the normal bus. It is a replacement. Something must have happened to the normal bus, as I thought. Not necessarily something terrible, though. Probably something minor that can be fixed in a day.

Probably.

The replacement bus looks older than the normal bus, but I'm sure it's fine.

The bus has pulled up.

I'm going to get on.

Many concerning things have happened in the short trip from the sidewalk to my seat. I am having a difficult time keeping my head right now, but I will do what you've said doctor, and try to analyze each of them in turn. Make small adjustments until I am well again.

First, there is a new bus driver to go along with the new bus. He is an old man. Very old. So old that I can't help but wonder whether or not he will be capable of seeing in the dark well enough to get us to the depot safely. I keep imagining the bus in a myriad of terrible accidents. I am picturing the other passengers burning, broken, screaming.

Dead.

I am picturing myself that way too.

I have to remember that the city would not allow him to work unless he was qualified. I must trust in the city to keep the best interests of its citizens in mind when making decisions such as replacing a missing bus driver, much as I so easily assumed earlier that the bus—this old bus with its old driver—was chosen because it was a suitable replacement for the good bus.

Sorry, normal. The normal bus. Not "good." I need to remember to use better language. You will have to forgive me doctor, but I am having a hard time right now.

I'm sure everything will be fine.

Secondly, there is a buzzy-faced man in my usual spot. I had to sit across from where I normally do.

I use the term buzzy-faced because, as we have discussed and as I've said, I am trying to use better language and it is nicer than saying that he is drunk.

As you know doctor, I have a particularly hard time with drunks. Drunks can be loud, belligerent, angry, and violent. Drunks can cause all kinds of problems due to these qualities, not the least of which is severe bodily harm and even death.

I guess I knew in the back of my mind that I would eventually run into drunks once I changed over to nights. But since everyone in the city changes over at the same time I figured that most of those who switch from days to nights would curb those kinds of impulses for a bit longer. I suppose the buzzy-faced man couldn't hold out.

He doesn't appear to be threatening. Right now he is slumped over, staring toward the front of the bus. He is coughing and scratching himself. He is thin, and his dirty clothes are too big for him. I think he might be one of the homeless. If that is the case, I suppose a liquor licensure is apt for his assignment. I imagine that when you have to live on the street until the next changeover, turning everything into one long blur probably makes it easier. Especially if you have to do it at night.

We all have our cures. I with my therapy, and the buzzy-faced man with his drink. We at least have that much in common. Different licensures, same result.

Just to be clear, doctor, I'm not comparing you to a bartender. Your help is, of course, much more effective and long-lasting than being a drunk.

I am thankful to have it.

Lastly, because this is a different bus, I cannot focus on the penny that is stuck to the floor like I usually do. This means I will have to positively orient myself in some other way tonight, for there are no interesting things on this floor to look at. I guess I could look at the buzzy-faced man's filthy shoes, but I'm afraid that if I do that maybe it might cause him to strike up a conversation with me. I am in no way ready for a step like that.

Especially not tonight.

I am sure I can find something to focus on.

I am sure everything will be fine.

Mrs. McClusky is not on the bus. You must remember me telling you about sweet old Mrs. McClusky, doctor, the spinster with the five cats. Well, she's not on the bus, and I'm very worried about her. Not only because she's not on the bus, but because she's not on the bus, yet her things are.

Sitting in the seat where Mrs. McClusky should be is her wooden-handled purse, and a plastic bag with her groceries in it. I can see two cans of "Feisty Cat" along with some beets and carrots through the plastic. Definitely her things. No doubt about it.

I may have only known her a little over half a month, doctor, but since the changeover she's been one of the few bright spots in my life, besides my visits with you, of course. She's always so friendly, so kind, and I look forward to the chats we sometimes have, when I'm feeling up to them. And I love that she always seems to know when I'm having one of my challenging days, because she never bothers me on those occasions.

She's a good woman, and right now the voice of fear is screaming her name.

I know you'd probably say that I'm getting too far ahead of myself, but I've run through this several times already. I honestly can't think of a good reason why Mrs. McClusky's things might be on the bus without her there to hold them. Maybe the reason the bus was so late wasn't just because they had to replace the normal bus, but also because Mrs. McClusky had some kind of medical emergency that required them to carry her off. The bus was over twenty minutes late and medical response units are averaging under eight minutes citywide, more than enough time for one to be called, respond, and carry Mrs. McClusky off on a stretcher.

I'm trying to make an adjustment to this line of thinking, to quiet the voice of fear, but I simply cannot find a positive way to spin this development.

What if she's dead?

What if it's worse than that?

What if this part of town has been...

No, it can't be that. I must not devolve into believing in rumors. I know that. I shouldn't even bring them up.

Please doctor, overlook this moment of weakness. I know it is wrong to indulge in unsavory rumors about the city. I know they aren't true, of course. It's just, you hear about people disappearing enough and you start to wonder, that's all. But wondering can get you into trouble since it can lead you so far away from the truth, which is often mundane enough as to be positively boring, as you've often pointed out.

It is comforting to think about it like that.

I am going to do my breathing exercises and try not to look at Mrs. McClusky's things. Since I don't have my penny, I will look out the window and count the street signs as they pass, as you suggested last week.

I did also notice Mrs. McClusky's flower scarf crushed beneath her purse.

I am sure everything will be fine.

The buzzy-faced man got off the bus. I wouldn't make note of it, except he did something very odd.

At first I was happy to see him pull the rope and call for a stop. I was glad I wouldn't have to worry about him or what he might do anymore, but after the bus came to a halt and he got up to exit through the rear door, he did something completely unexpected. He stopped by Mrs. McClusky's things and gathered them up before stepping off the bus. And as the bus was leaving, while I watched him through the window, completely at a loss, he smiled at me, and then winked!

I don't know what to make of this, doctor. Why should this dirty drunk have anything to do with sweet old Mrs. McClusky? I can't imagine that he does, so did he merely decide to steal her things on a whim? Was he tasked during this changeover not only with homelessness but with thievery as well? I guess that would make sense, drunks do often do unpredictable and morally irresponsible things. He would have to play the part convincingly, I suppose.

But why the wave and the wink?

Does he know something that I don't about my situation, or did he merely catch me glancing at Mrs. McClusky's things over and over and notice my confusion? Did he then decide to take them in order to confound me for fun? That would certainly be something that an unpredictable drunk might do. Perhaps this is merely part of his assignment, putting those around him off their game. Perhaps this is a new challenge to those of us living normal lives in this district.

It has been two years since the ordinance was passed, and the buzzy-faced man was the first homeless person I've encountered, not to mention the first drunk.

Is this a new phase in the plan?

I suppose things can't always be perfect, not all changes can be good. The city planners know this. How can one be expected to grow without being challenged?

Weren't we just discussing that, doctor?

This has been a challenging night, so far, let me tell you. My routines have been upset to an alarming degree, but I think I am up to it. We should be getting to the depot soon anyway, and not long after that I will be home, safe in my apartment.

This thought brings me much comfort.

Maybe the buzzy-faced man is being a good citizen and returning Mrs. McClusky's things to her. This district has always been a good place to live with good people living in it. I could be worrying for nothing. That is, after all, the reason I am seeing you, doctor. I am going to keep that in mind for the rest of the ride.

I am sure everything is okay.

I am sure everything will be fine.

This is getting really out of hand.

A man got on the bus a few stops after the buzzy-faced man departed, another homeless by my reckoning, and sat near the front of the bus, near the driver. He is very large, and is wearing several layers of clothing. He resembles a great trash heap, if I'm being honest. He smells like one too. I know this shouldn't bother me, and after surviving the ordeal of the buzzy-faced man I'm sure it wouldn't have, but there are several things about this new bum that stand out as concerning.

First he has been whispering back and forth with the driver since he sat down. I think they know each other. I'm almost sure of it. The way they are whispering and laughing quietly together looks too familiar to think anything less. I hate to use the word "conspiratorially," but no other description fits their behavior better, I'm afraid.

Also, I'm almost positive that whatever it is they are talking about has to do with me.

I know you'd probably chalk this up to my paranoia getting the better of me, but I promise you doctor that the big homeless man has been shifting his eyes back at me over and over when he thinks I'm not looking. He even pointed once, right at me. It couldn't have been any of the other passengers because the last of them departed at the stop immediately before he arrived on the bus. I'm now wondering if their leaving had something to do with my current predicament.

I'm sorry I characterized it that way, doctor, but I can't help but think that that is the truth of it.

I am in a predicament.

It feels good to at least acknowledge it. Write it out loud, so to speak. It makes me feel much better, actually. Strange that it should work like that. Maybe you can explain it to me in our next session, doctor.

Maybe the big homeless man is a friend of the driver. Maybe they shared common shifts before the last changeover. Maybe they—

The driver just announced over the radio—an odd choice seeing as there are now only two passengers—that the bus will be taking an alternate route to the depot. He said this will add "significant time" to our route.

We've picked up speed. The bus lurched alarmingly and I nearly fell over in my seat. I think I saw the large homeless man laugh.

I'm having a hard time, doctor. I'm going to try and keep writing but I'm not sure I can concentrate on—

He just let two more homeless on the bus. They sat up front with the other one, near the driver.

I looked out the window when we stopped and I don't recognize anything. I've taken alternate routes before, but never to anyplace that looks like this. My district is humble, but clean. The buildings are always free of graffiti and refuse. We take pride in keeping it that way, yet these buildings look abused and abandoned. They have boarded-up windows and doors, like heads with bandaged eyes and mouths.

The lights are fluttery here, too.

I guess I always knew places like this must exist in the city, but I never imagined having to travel to one—

The bus lurched again. I dropped my pen. The new homeless laughed along with the large one and the driver. They are together now.

He's let more on. A group this time, about four, by my count, but it's hard to tell as they all mesh together so seamlessly. Their clothes appear different, yet they might as well be wearing uniforms for how similar they look, like shades of the street. They sit up near the other group and begin chattering along with them. The sound of their conversation buzzes all around me. I'd put my hands on the sides of my head to ward it off, but then I couldn't keep writing about my predicament, and right now this is the only thing that is helping.

What are they talking about?

Why is it so funny?

What does it have to do with me?

More homeless now, too many to count before they merged with the other group. The smell is becoming unbearable. They account for more than half the bus now. The nearest of them is bordering Mrs. McClusky's seat.

My head is swimming, and it feels like I'm in the center of a tornado. I am a sweaty fist, clenched in place. Between the odor, the constant start and stop of the bus, and the panic raging inside I feel like I might pass out, or vomit all over myself.

The bus just turned down a street where the lights are no longer fluttery. They've all gone out.

I can't make out anything anymore.

I have never felt more lost.

I feel boxed in. I'm going to move to the back of the bus to get some space.

Why are we going so fast?

I'm now sitting all the way in the back, on the bench that faces directly toward the front. I can survey things from here.

After thinking it all over, I have come to the conclusion that this has to be coordinated. Some kind of test, or an experiment, perhaps. I know what you said about the rumors, doctor, but you must admit that this is all very unordinary.

I'm not stupid, doctor. Or crazy.

The late bus. The new driver. Mrs. McClusky. The drunk who stole her things. The change in route. The homeless mob who won't stop talking about me, laughing at me. This can't be happenstance.

This is a pre-planned predicament.

I see now how my life since the changeover could have been designed to lead up to this moment. Of course Mrs. McClusky and I would be fast friends considering what happened with my grandmother. Of course my new coworkers on nights would constantly yammer on about strange rumors dealing with disused portions of the city, about people disappearing, subjects which would naturally upset me. Of course I would fill this notebook up, along with our sessions, with garbage thoughts and worries about those rumors. And of course, like telling a child not to eat a cookie or play with a sharp object, you would advise me not to allow these rumors to warp my thinking about how I regarded the new changeover.

Of course, that was all I would do.

Are you in on it, doctor?

Have I been chosen by the city?

Are you my therapist, or my handler?

I guess at this point it does not matter. I am involved, whether I choose to be or not.

It feels good to admit that.

This being the case I think it might be wise of me to do something unpredictable. Something my citizen profile would not indicate as even a remote possibility.

Something you would certainly never see coming.

I am going to pull the rope.

I am going to get off the bus.

I'm on the street now. The bus has gone. I'm standing directly beneath one of those "You Are the City, and the City is YOU!" billboards they have flashing all over.

This is all the light I could find.

I pulled the rope, and at first I was worried the driver wouldn't stop. They all went silent when the bell sounded, turned and looked directly at me. They watched as I gathered my things in a rush. The driver drove through three stops while they stared.

I almost suffocated.

He finally stopped and they all got up at once, began moving toward the end of the bus. I threw myself out of the seat and lunged toward the back door. I fell against it, banging my knee real good. It was all I could do to stop myself from beating against the back door, screaming to be let out.

I was certain the time had come for the experiment to end, but the driver opened the door and I tumbled out onto the concrete.

Turning over I looked up and saw the crowd dispersed across the windows of the bus, piled on one another, their grimy faces and hands smashed into glass.

Every one of them was laughing, even the driver, their jaws moving up and down, their teeth not touching.

And then the bus was gone.

And I am not sure where I am.

I feel better to be off the bus, but I am not sure that I have escaped.

Beyond the light beneath the billboard is nothing short of Void. Up and down this street the buildings are caving in. There are shadows crouched on shadows where the brickwork has failed and collapsed. Great, black holes surround me.

There are things moving in and out of them. I am sure of it.

The billboard lights are fluttering.

You have to help me.

I am not sure I can still trust you, doctor, but right now, your words are all I have.

It is okay that it is dark.

It is okay that I am alone.

I am sure the rumors are just rumors.

I am sure that there is nothing out there.

I am sure I will get home safely.

I am sure everything will be—

Something's Off About Wizzle

Brian eased into the men's bathroom and closed the door behind him. He locked it.

Turning to face the urinals against the wall, he counted five before coming to the one currently servicing the thing he'd followed in.

"Wizzle," he said, shaking. "We're going to resolve this once and for all."

Wizzle finished up and wobbled to the side, his face stretched by an empty smile. As always, his weirdly roving, bulgy eyes chilled Brian to the bone.

"Well, look who it is! Whadda ya say pal?" said Wizzle in that awful, fluttery voice.

Brian nearly lost his nerve. That voice...

"I say...I say Wizzle isn't a man's name."

"Well, that's what my momma always called me, so I guess it's the name of this one!" Wizzle laughed, poking himself cartoonishly in the chest with both thumbs, elbows out like chicken wings.

"How about this then," said Brian, lowering his voice and advancing. "I say Wizzle isn't a hu-*man* name. Now, 'whadda ya say' about that, *pal?*"

"That's a strange joke, buddy. I don't get it," said Wizzle, folding his rubbery mouth into a perplexed wave. His eyes rolled in their sockets, giving Brian another jolt up the spine.

"Your bullshit about medical conditions doesn't fool me. I've been watching you, and I've figured it out. I know why you have plastic skin, and cartoon eyes. I know why you sound like someone straight out of some old comic. You're pretending to be one of us, but you aren't. You're something else, and I'm gonna show everyone the TRUTH!"

Brian lunged, grabbing Wizzle by the hair, pulling hard. It felt like greased yarn, nearly slipping through his fingers.

Wizzle screeched inhumanly, and Brian almost let go. But he didn't. He knew he might never get this chance again. Instead, he gritted his teeth, clenched his fist, and pulled harder, harder. Wizzle screamed again, louder, louder. His warped, warbly screeching turned Brian's stomach. It was the sound of clowny murder.

Suddenly, there was a soft *pop*, and something gave. Brian tumbled to the ground. He unfolded his hands, looked into them, and saw that he was clutching a rubbery wad of hair and human features. Even then, with the truth bare faced and facing him, he couldn't believe it. He slowly raised widened eyes.

Wizzle was hunched over, turned away, with both hands covering the back of his head. He began cackling, low and sinister at first, then faster, faster, faster into hysterics. He turned, drawing himself up to his full height, fully exposing his true face.

Brian felt a warm wetness spread beneath him.

The truth he so wanted, that he'd come into the bathroom just minutes before determined to uncover, was beyond imagining. Before him stood an impossible horror, one of globular, painted eyeballs and multicolored fur. One with a wide, flat mouth that split its round head in ridiculous, flapping motions as it laughed. It was a face of Saturday mornings, of toy aisles and coloring books; children's play and imagination. It belonged in those places where songs were sung about the alphabet and counting, where kids learned how to share, and play pretend. It did not belong where it was in that moment, springing out of the neck of a rumpled suit, five-fingered man flesh poking out of its sleeves.

Brian was frozen; speechless as Wizzle squatted down in front of him.

"No one will ever believe you," said Wizzle, plucking the person mask from Brian's slack hands, before tugging it back on. Tufts of puppet pelt peeked through the eyeholes as he ghoulishly contorted it into place. Brian sat insane within the spectacle. Then, Wizzle smiled that ridiculous smile one more time, then screamed for help.

As the police dragged poor, howling Brian away, Sheila from accounting patted Wizzle on the shoulder.

"He was always going on about you. I guess we should have seen this coming," she said.

"I just hope he gets the help he needs," said Wizzle, discreetly pushing a stray clump of rainbow fluff into his collar.

Where We Are, Where We Were, and Where We Will Always Be

We are being driven by a car made of meat down a road composed of squashed marigolds and the eyes of rabbits. The buildings around us are rubberized, metallicized, or melting into pools of ice cream. A man runs by, his face twisted into a silent wail, skin bubbling with the faces of a thousand plastic babies. There are people fused to the sidewalk, their bodies slowly turning to concrete. Others struggle and flail while sinking slowly into puddles of black morass. The smell of warm licorice fills the car, briefly casting out the stench of rotten, burning pork that wafts in from the vehicle's fleshy engine.

I shudder to think what it's using for gas.

The puppet still dominates the sky. Clara says it remains the same for her; same black suit, same wooden limbs and painted-on face. To me, it looks like one of those fuzzy, sleevey things that psychiatrists use to get little kids to show them where their uncles touched them.

Clara's moving further away, becoming more presence than person.

The longer this goes on, the more unreal she feels, even though she's sitting right there, squishing up out of the seat, craning her head out the window to get a better look at the puppet to see if it's still there. It is. She's sitting there doing that, but she might as well be inside a painting, or in a television show. Like everything else, she's becoming chimerical, as foreign as the tiny orcas raining from the sky and spattering against the windshield, or the slimy mucus that seeps out of the steering wheel moving itself inside my hands.

I'm not sure where the car is taking us, or if we'll even be in the same car when we get there. Maybe, by that time, it won't be Clara next to me. Maybe it'll be you. I'm not sure how this works. Why can you hear me, see me? Are you the one doing this? If you aren't, then for your sake I hope you don't end up here. I hope, for your sake, you stay right where you are. I have this feeling that as long as you're there, I'm safe.

But if you were here...

I was the first to notice. Clara and I had gone to some dirtbag motel off the interstate to celebrate one of those anniversaries that's really a monthiversary (Clara's idea, of course) and the original plan was to smoke, screw, sleep, and eat to our heart's content. I was flush, and Clara was keen to spend every dollar I had to my name. I didn't mind. She was one hell of a distraction, as far as distractions go, and I could think of a lot worse things to do than drop all my cash on a weekend of debauchery with the highest-earning nighttime act at the Purple Armadillo.

Anyway, I woke up close to midnight to a call of nature, and noticed this weird light flashing from the edges of the blackout curtains. At first I thought it might be cops or something, but the colors were all wrong. Green, purple, orange; not cop colors at all, so I pulled back the curtains and took a peek.

The colors were everywhere, touched *everything*, like the sky was full of burning candy. I opened the door to get a better look, and the colors flooded the room. And I don't mean that they came in like normal light. No, these colors flowed past and around me like smoke swirling through a projector beam.

Clara grunted and opened her eyes, told me to shut the door before seeing the smoke light and bolting upright in the bed. She sat there waving her arms in front of her dreamily, running her fingers through the cloud, splitting it into soft tendrils over and over. I watched her, transfixed, her nude form bathed in kaleidoscope.

Hard as it was, I turned away, wandered outside in my boxers. There was a small group gathered in the center of the parking lot, their faces turned upward, mouths gaping. I joined them, lifting my own head to see what they were gawking at. I nearly fell over from shock.

There was a rip in the sky. The starfield had been torn open, revealing a churning, white Void from which the colors were bleeding.

Being birthed from this Void was a giant puppet's head; wriggling, thrashing, working its jaws silently up and down, like a great, yarny worm burrowing its way free from some extra-dimensional prison.

At some point Clara, wrapped in the comforter, touched my elbow, breaking me out of a minutes-long reverie. Without hesitation I grabbed her wrist and led her back into the hotel, locking the door behind us.

I stood with my head against the door, my back to the room. Clara's breaths behind me were ragged and heavy to match my own. Turning, the first thing I saw was that she had gotten dressed, but then noticed her arm outstretched, finger pointing at the wall in front of the bed. I looked to see that instead of a television resting precariously upon a dilapidated old dresser, there was instead a set of chrome elevator doors.

I barely managed a clumsy "What the hell?" before Clara started toward the doors hypnotically, lining her pointing finger up with the call button resting beside those impossible doors.

"No!" I cried, reaching for her, but my feet sank into the floor as if it were made of sponge. I fell headfirst into the carpet, sinking several inches down. She pressed the button. A loud whirring sounded. The doors opened with a warbled ping. Multicolored light tumbled out.

She turned and looked down at me. "What are you doing?" she asked, her voice trancelike. "We have to go." She stepped into the elevator, pressing her hand against the side to prevent the doors from closing.

My mind wouldn't focus. I couldn't form words. There was nothing but to follow, so I did.

The inside of the elevator was glass, and beyond the panes was our city, irrevocably changed. Skyscrapers pulsed like parasitic worms escaping from the eyes of a dead snail. The streets flowed like liquid, lapping up and over their curbs. People were gathered, standing ankle-deep in those streets, every one of them gazing skyward. I looked up with them, just as I had done in the parking lot, to once again see the puppet dominating the sky, its sock-like body undulating as well, its mouth constantly working.

A calm came over me, like one feels when dreaming, confronted by things that cannot be real, yet are accepted as such. "This must be a dream," I said to Clara, who laughed.

"Can't be a dream. I'm here too," she said, through her mirth.

"That doesn't prove anything."

She just kept giggling.

"Why are you laughing?" I asked her, but she kept going.

The elevator doors closed, and we began to descend. Clara pressed her whole body against the glass, looking up and down and side to side manically. I had a vivid notion of her falling through—cut to ribbons, tumbling to her death—and tried to pull her away, but she wouldn't budge. She jerked her elbow from my grip and continued to work her head spasmodically.

"The puppet, it's Zilch!" she said.

"Who?"

"Zilch the Strange, from the Dr. Buttons Show."

"I don't know what that is," I replied.

"He was Dr. Buttons's sidekick. I watched that show every afternoon after school when I was a kid. I used to love the silly way Zilch laughed. *Hyuck, hyuck, hyuck, Dr. B.* You never watched Dr. Buttons?"

"No," I said, trying to pull her away again.

"You really missed out, then."

She pulled herself out of my hand once more.

The elevator stopped, the doors opened. We both turned and looked through the portal to see the bullpen of a large office, akin to the inside of a call center. Hundreds of unmanned telephones rested on desks that seemed to go on forever. Chairs were scattered, computer monitors upturned, some hanging off their desks, CRT heads cleaved from digital bodies. Paper littered every surface. Shreds of it danced in the air. It was as though a bomb had gone off.

Clara finally peeled herself off the elevator window. We stepped into the office together. The doors closed behind us, and when I looked back, they were gone, nothing but a blank wall where they had been.

"I used to work here," said Clara.

"You what? When?"

"Right after I dropped out of college. My uncle got me the job." She ran away from me, across the room and down one of the exploded aisles. "This was my station. We cold-called people, tried to sell them security systems." She reached down, picked up the receiver of the workstation's phone, put it to her ear. "Good evening, Mr. Whats-i-doo. Sorry to interrupt your dinner, but would you be interested in scheduling an appointment with one of our top-notch, home security experts today?" Clara dropped the handset, started giggling like an idiot again.

Every phone in the office went off at once. Over and over they rang, until Clara retrieved the receiver and placed it back to the side of her head.

"Hello," she said quietly.

The phone speakers buzzed to life. A high, thin, staticky voice blasted out of them. "Dr. Buttons is retiring today. There's cake in the break room. Come and get it. I repeat, there's break in the cake room, a break in the cake room. Come get your fill before it's too late. Hyuck, hyuck, hyuck."

"Zilch..." said Clara, then dashed away toward the back of the office.

"Wait!" I cried, and chased after.

She ran down several interconnected hallways—left, then right, then left again, over and over—filled with doors and frosted windows. Shadowy, wavy forms inside the offices pressed smudgy faces and hands against the cloudy glass. Indistinct chatter poured out from behind the doors; one long, muddied conversation that oozed into my ears and left my head addled.

Finally, we reached the end of our mad dash. Clara stood before a door at the dead end of the last hallway. A banner hung across the door with the words *"Retyremint Partee!!!"* smeared across it in red paint. Four-fingered handprints surrounded the misspelled scrawl.

"This is it," she said. "The cake room." She opened the door.

That description proved to be more than apt. Inside, the room was top to bottom covered in icing. The smell was sickening, cloying. I retched. I could see several dozen fully clothed mannequins gathered in a semi-circle, their blank faces posed to look down on something obscured by Clara's body.

Clara stepped in without hesitation, her feet instantly sinking into the confection, all the way up to her ankles. She raised her knees, pulling her feet out one at a time with a quiet sucking sound, and made her way over to a table resting in the center of the room. I followed, stepping carefully. The spaces between my toes filled with cold icing and warm cake.

I joined Clara beside the table. On top of it lay the body of a balding, middle-aged man dressed in a brown suit. His arms were crossed over his chest, and his eyes were closed behind round, wire-rimmed glasses.

"My Uncle Bernard," she half-whispered, touching the lapel tentatively.

"The one who got you the job?"

"Yeah. But he died last year. He looked just like this when they laid him out."

"I'm sorry," I replied stupidly.

"Don't be. He was a piece of shit. Used to babysit me for my mother after school. Take me down into his basement to 'play' after my cartoons. Sick fuck." She snorted, and then spit a green glob onto the face of the body. Its skin distorted as the phlegmy discharge ran down. Without thinking, I reached out to touch the distortion, but she grabbed my hand.

"Don't. It's just icing; more cake."

The mannequin closest to us, one dressed in a black tuxedo, raised its hand, which had a silver cake server taped to it.

"I guess you get to cut the cake," I said.

Clara smacked the hand of the mannequin, dislodging its arm, which slid out of the sleeve and splattered onto the cake floor. She screamed, bringing both her fists up above her head. She pushed them together at the wrists, and then smashed them down into the head of the cake corpse, exploding it into pieces of red and pink. She scooped handfuls of the body out, threw them at the mannequins over and over, until every one was askew and the Uncle Bernard cake was nothing more than a mass of baked gore.

A speaker in the upper-left corner of the room exploded with the sound of the voice from the telephone, the one Clara identified as "Zilch."

"Now, now, you cow. Gifts are supposed to be enjoyed, not destroyed. But it's okay if you don't want to play. Someone else can take a turn. Hyuck, hyuck, hyuck."

The floor gave way beneath us, and we were sucked into a cakehole to tumble through a howling, black abyss.

Eventually, I landed hard on my back, elbow deep in grass. Above me, the puppet was there, still working its sock mouth.

"Must be one big foot," I said deliriously and laughed.

"What do you mean," asked Clara from my right.

I sat up, seeing that we were lying in a large open field dotted with marigolds.

"The puppet, it kind of looks like a big sock. I was just thinking about how big a foot must have gone in it once."

"It's not a sock. It's Zilch. He's a ventriloquist's dummy."

I looked up again, and back to Clara. "Looks like a sock to me."

"You're wrong."

"Whatever. It's different for me, I guess." I stood up, stretched, then ran my feet back and forth in the grass, attempting to get as much icing and cake off as I could.

Clara stood up as well. "Where are we now?"

I gave it another survey. It took me no time to realize.

"Rabbit Run."

"Rabbit Run?"

"Yeah. I used to spend summers here with my Grandpa Willy. After my grandma died, he moved out to the country. Called his place Rabbit Run, because of all the wild rabbits on the land. He used to take me out to hunt them. 'To keep 'em off the flowers,' he said. Don't really have a stomach for killing, though. Could never pull the trigger. He called me Little Pussy my whole life because of it."

"So he was an asshole?"

"Yeah. Used to stand behind me while I aimed, then crack me on the head with his knuckles when I wouldn't shoot."

I turned in a circle, looking for Grandpa Willy's house, but it wasn't there. Instead, on the horizon, was a concrete structure far in the distance, stretching tall and ominous.

"I guess we go there."

"Sure. What else?" she said, shrugging.

We'd barely taken a step before the ground churned around us; exploded. Grass and dirt flew into the air and rained down on our heads. The air fluttered with yellow petals. Thousands of decaying rabbit bodies pulled themselves up and out of the ground, began scrabbling around the field. A crack resounded through the air, unmistakable. A gunshot.

"Run, rabbits. RUN!" Grandpa Willy. Behind us.

We both turned to look, and there he was, looming at the edge of the distant treeline. He stood half as tall as the tallest of those trees, twelve feet if he was an inch, dressed just like I remember: overalls without a shirt, an overlarge hat covering his head, and of course, no shoes or socks to be found. "Just as the good Lord intended," he used to say.

Delirium overtook me at the sight of my giant grandfather. "Big foot," I said again, and laughed, though I still don't know why.

He aimed his enormous rifle in our direction.

"I said run, Little Pussy! Take your bitch and get to gettin'."

"I think we should do what he says," said Clara, over the squeals of the dead rabbits. She grabbed at my arm, pulled it hard.

"Nah, he's a shit shot," I said, still drunk on whatever spell the place had put me under. "We got time."

Another crack, and a giant bullet wooshed past us, exploding the bodies of about ten undead bunnies as it hit the ground with a loud "WUMPH."

This broke me out of my stupor.

"Okay, let's go," I said.

And we were running.

The ground boiled around our ankles. Rabbit bones melted together into a tar-like consistency, slurping as we sank into it. I could feel wet teeth scratching against my shins, gooey eyeballs popping under my heels. We had to pull one another out of the muck several times. Giant bullets shattered the air and field in front of us. At one point, I dared to look over my shoulder. Grandpa Willy strode not far behind, his legs lengthening impossibly with each extension. Those great, bare feet of his slapped the ground. I could see bits and pieces of liquified rabbit carcasses and marigolds stuck between his toes, dripping onto the ground in black, red, and yellow blobs.

"Gonna getcha," he cried, raising his gun once more and letting another blast fly, which I could feel against my ear as it passed and landed just inches in front of us. "Gonna get me a Little Pussy. Two for the price of one! Hyuck, hyuck, hyuck."

I picked Clara up, threw her over my shoulder, then pumped my way through the rabbity quagmire as hard as I could, desperately trying to reach the concrete behemoth looming larger and larger at the end of the field. Somehow I knew if I managed that, ol' Willy couldn't follow.

Clara, bouncing on my shoulder, eyes no doubt increasingly full of my grandfather, kept yelling "Hurry," as if I didn't already know, and just when I thought I could feel Willy's hot breath and tobacco spit on my neck, my feet came down on solid asphalt.

I sat Clara down, turned in a circle, only to find no Willy, no dead rabbit field; nothing but dreadful silence, and an expanse of parking spaces that went on into forever—a solid gray horizon; the concrete building its only feature, rupturing out of the ground like a tumor. The building was cube shaped, and windowless, except for a set of double red doors in its center. There were no markings to indicate what type of building it was. Its true nature scratched at my brain, needled me with ghostly memory.

Without thinking, I looked to the sky. The puppet was there, socky jaws working, the only constant in the now inconstant world.

I plucked an eyeball from Clara's shoulder, and flicked it onto the ground. She laughed, quietly, and put a hand on my cheek. Rubbing her thumb and forefinger across, she brought them away: there were two tiny buck teeth, pinched between her nails. I laughed along with her. Staring at one another we let our laughter overtake us for a bit— what else could we do?—before finally turning our attention to the structure.

We approached the doors cautiously. Clara grabbed one handle, I the other. We pulled them open at the same time.

The air that rushed out to meet us was stagnant, with a fake floral finish. The kind of air you might find inside an old woman's apartment, or the vestibule of a dying hotel. I couldn't make out what waited beyond; the inside was too dim. Clara stepped in first, disappeared into the darkness. I briefly entertained the insane idea of closing the doors behind her, consigning her to whatever fate awaited within that dully familiar place; but of course, I followed, if only because I seemed to have no other choice.

It took my eyes a moment to adjust. I blinked over and over until the room polaroided itself into sense. I found myself in a waiting room full of hard plastic orange chairs welded together at their bases. Sitting in these chairs were dolls, ragamuffins, the kind you sometimes see kids playing with in old movies. Some were slumped, heads forward, between their legs; others to the side, arms over their chests, legs splayed out in front. Each doll was the size you'd expect from something designed for a child, except one. In the far-right corner was one of full human size. It sat rigid, stumpy hands holding a clipboard, half the wooly brown hair intermittently missing from its head. The doll in the seat next was reaching across, clutching onto its leg. Its head rested on the lap of the bigger doll.

A cold chill ran down my spine. I knew them. I remembered them. I was there so many times. The big doll was my grandmother. The little one, me: my shiny Buster Browns dangling over the seat, my red wagon overalls buttoned on only one side, just like I liked it. This was the waiting room of the place my granny used to go for chemotherapy. She would bring me along since my mother worked during the day. Tears welled in my eyes. I had an overwhelming urge to go and throw the little doll out of its chair and take its place, to clutch onto my granny again after all these years. Instead, I turned to Clara.

She was on the ground, on her knees. Her face was ashen. Her mouth moved up and down without sound, reminding me of the puppet. I squatted, grabbed her shoulders.

"What's wrong?"

"Do you know where this is?" she asked me, looking into my eyes with an emotion somewhere between anger and shame.

"I do. This is where my grandmother came for chemo, for all the good it did her."

"No, that's not right. This is the waiting room of Patterson Women's Health Clinic, Dunnstown North."

"The...wait, what? No, this is St. Bartholomew's Cancer Center in Kingsport."

She grabbed my arms and stood up.

"What color is the wallpaper?" she asked.

"No wallpaper. The walls are painted beige."

"There is wallpaper. Baby blue with yellow flowers. I'll never forget it."

"So we're seeing it differently, like the puppet."

"I guess so."

She walked around the room slowly, touching the backs of every chair. She sat down in one, right on top of a doll, like it wasn't there. The doll squished and then popped with a puff of air, disappearing beneath her.

I joined her, picking up the blond-haired doll in the chair beside her. I set it gently on the floor.

"So, a cancer hospital for me, and an abortion clinic for you. That's just...that's..."

"Fucking sick, is what it is. This is all one big, sick joke. First that job with my uncle, and now this."

"You don't see the dolls, do you?"

"Dolls?"

"There's dolls in all the chairs. There's even one over in the corner that looks like my granny, and one beside her that looks like me."

She glanced over at where I pointed.

"No, the chairs are empty."

"Ahhh. See, they were always full when I was here. I used to sit and think about all those people being sick, like my grandmother. I wondered if they had kids who would miss them too."

"I was never lonelier than I was in this room, sitting by myself," said Clara, wiping her eyes and nose with the back of her sleeve.

Clara grabbed my hand, held it against her face. I put my head against hers, kissed her cheek. We sat there like that, comforting each other in pain long passed and found again—until a loud voice blared out over the intercom.

"*Calling Doctor Howard, Doctor Fine, Doctor Howard. I repeat: calling Doctor Howard, Doctor Fine, Doctor Howard. Hyuck, hyuck, hyuck.*"

"It's mocking us," I said.

"FUCK YOU!" Clara screamed at the ceiling.

The door beside the empty reception desk opened, and a figure came through. Its body was human shaped, wearing a crisp, white lab coat over a brown suit, but the head was decidedly not human. It was the head of the puppet, giant sock face sticking out of the collar, googly eyes rolling.

Zilch.

"No, no. Fuck youuuuuuu!" said Zilch, pointing at Clara. Then it laughed, and laughed, and laughed, holding its belly with one arm while keeping its other up and pointing.

Behind it, then, ducking through the doorway, came two hulking nurses. They advanced on us slowly, their round, shiny heads and black, featureless faces like unfinished drawings. Clara stood up and started toward them, an insane fury in her eyes, but I could see crushing death in their fat, four-fingered hands, so I shot after her, grabbed her, pulled her around the brutes, who awkwardly lunged to stop us. We bowled through the sock doctor, pushing it into the wall. It was still laughing as I ran through the door, deeper into the offices. Clara, in tow, was still screaming a practically incoherent stream of profanities over her shoulder.

Doors upon doors zoomed by as we ran. There were voices coming from behind them that sounded like someone talking when you're not listening. It was the same murky conversation as before, back in the hallways of Clara's old office. It sounded as if it was getting closer, both in distance and comprehension. I was instantly afraid of what would happen should I ever understand what those voices were saying.

The hallway ended in a stairwell, and Clara pushed past me to go through when I hesitated. She made it halfway down the first flight before turning around.

"What are you doing? We have to go!" she said.

I couldn't move.

"What if it's worse?" I asked.

"What if what's worse?"

"Whatever is down there. Another sock-headed man, a cake room, melting rabbits, giant grandpas, rooms with wallpaper and no wallpaper at the same time. Christ, Clara, I don't think I can bear any more."

She eased back up the stairs and grabbed my hands.

"We're still together. We're still real. That's something, right?"

I nodded, slowly.

"Then let's go. Whatever it is, we'll face it together, okay?"

I took a deep breath. "Okay."

We started down the stairs.

The stairwell was fairly normal, thankfully. The only thing was that it became narrower, the deeper we went. At first, I tried to convince myself that I was imagining it, but we kept descending, flight after flight, until I began to feel that when we reached the bottom, we might be greeted by hell itself. Eventually, though, we did reach the end, and huddled together in front of a tall door marked "Exit," on a step that was no more than a foot and a half wide. Just like before, we looked at one another, and then, as one, opened the door.

On the other side was a vast, empty place, walls and floors made of pulsating pink flesh, containing car-like things made of the same.

This is when I first felt you.

Clara let go of my hand, wandered away from me. That is when we disconnected completely.

I could feel myself being watched; prickles on the back of the neck, scalp tingling, filled with an overwhelming urge to find the eyes I felt upon me. There was nothing and no one, just Clara and I in that strange, empty place that reminded me of a parking garage.

Clara moved to the nearest car, then opened its door.

"C'mon," she said, her voice far away.

My feet moved, and an awful sensation of not being in control came over me, as if my legs were being worked by invisible strings. I got in

the car, felt the cold, meaty seat against my bare skin. The door closed of
its own accord. The car started, rolled backward out of the parking space.

We were off.

Round and round we went, passing countless other meat cars, all
of which contained one or more passengers, all blurry and indistinct.
Upon reaching the end, we stopped at a structure that resembled
a ticket booth. Hanging out of the booth was a hamburger-faced
construction worker crammed into a jumpsuit, two giant plastic
googly eyes without pupils pressed into its soft head. It had a paper
sign around its neck, soaked in red, and the name "Stevie" scrawled
across it in uneven black letters. Its hand was out, four-fingered and
plump. A speaker by the thing's head buzzed and Zilch's voice came
through.

"Tickets puh-leeze, hyuck, hyuck, hyuck."

The glove box fell open. Two slices of an unrecognizable meat with
black squiggles all over fell out and onto Clara's lap. She handed them
to me, a strange glazed look in her eye, and I placed them, autonomi-
cally, into "Stevie's" meaty paw.

"Thanks a big ol' bunch. Now, buckle up, buckaroos!"

The car sped away, tires spinning, squelching, filling the cab with
the smell of cooked pork.

We pulled from the parking lot and into a great dark, fleshy tunnel,
just large enough for our car to pass through. Everything went black.
I lost sensation, could no longer feel the seat against my body. A sense
of non-being enveloped me. I tried to scream, to prove I still existed.
I couldn't.

My arms reached up and grabbed the steering wheel without me
asking them to. The sensation of its slimy solidity brought relief. That
I could feel something again emboldened me, and with great effort I
managed to wrest some control away from whatever force now domi-
nated me.

I whispered Clara's name, but she did not respond. I thought for sure she was no longer there.

The car began to slow, and I heard the sides squishing against the walls. The antiseptic reek of ozone began to mix with the coppery scent that permeated the interior of the strange vehicle. Then, there was a light; dull and yellow at first, then abruptly bright, blinding white.

We exited the tunnel—squeezed out with a *splorch*—and bounced onto the rabbit-eye, marigold road, back at the beginning and the end, right where we started, you and I.

We're nearly there now. The closer we get, the sense that we've done this before becomes stronger. My story repeated, again. I can feel you more with each passing minute, out there, listening to my words—which sound like your voice—inside that great dark abyss between your ears. Though your face may change, though you may not be the you you were when last we met, you're still the same as ever: a consumer, consuming me; creating me; torturing me.

Puppet and puppet master, keeping on and on.

The car detaches from the ground, rises into the sky, as it always does. The puppet is growing larger and larger in the windshield. A voice comes over the radio. It's good old Zilch, singing that same old song, a chestnut my father used to play for me during car rides on rare visits.

Welcome back, my friends, to the show that never ends. We're so glad you could attend. Come inside! Come inside.

How many times now?

How many more to go?

I look over to Clara and she's shimmering, off in her own strange story, no doubt. She's lost to me, of course. I wonder if I ever had her to begin with.

At least it isn't you. Like I said before, as long as it isn't, then I believe we both have a chance. As long as I'm in here, and you're out there, and the puppet isn't in your sky, I think we'll be okay.

But eventually it will come for you, like it came for us. It'll come and torture you with all the things you wish never were, force you to tell tumbled-together tragedies forever.

I know this because it's telling me to tell you. It thinks it's funny for you to know. Hyuck, hyuck, hyuck.

What will your puppet look like, I wonder?

I'm going in now. The sock mouth is open. The yarny darkness beckons.

Until next time, whoever you are.

in carnality

Across a plane of flesh, the mound of meat moved. Lurching, sloughing, absorbing, it roiled across the oozy surface, striving toward an instinctive but undetermined goal. Mindlessly, it melted and reformed ahead of itself, ever forward, traversing the landscape in the way of all meat, but also in a way unique to its particular grouping; tantalized in the knowing of each yard of newer meat, saddened by the losing of old meat to the new. Pausing for a moment in order to consider itself (as it often did) the mound briefly took the form of a thinking thing, and placed a finger-like protuberance upon the bloody, ghostly face its thinking made.

Where am I going? thought the mound. *Will I know when I get there? If all is meat, is always meat, then why move at all?* Good questions, it thought, and other meat that made it up answered back the same refrain it always offered in these moments.

Because we must, said the other meat.

I suppose that's true, thought the mound, and shrugging (or approximating such a motion) moved on.

As it made its way across the vast, meaty plain—which stretched out to all sides, touched all horizons—it came to know other mounds, similar to itself, in various states of being. Many of them careened along as it did, rooting toward whatever goal was waiting, and these kindred masses soothed the mound, as they showed it that it wasn't alone in its endeavor. It made play of trying to mimic their exact movements, synching its rhythms to theirs, gliding along to their time. It found calm in the shared experience.

Some were not mobile, but instead had become still; lost, possibly, in the same meaty contemplation it often found itself engaged in, or perhaps frozen in some kind of indecisive paralysis, looped within a recursive anxiety. The mound could not say. It merely moved, and moved, and moved.

Some had taken other forms, much different to it and its synchronic brethren, and to the immobile thinkers as well. Giant, ambling formations were these other forms, and they towered above the fleshy expanse, looming titanous. How they came to be so massive the mound had no idea, but it could feel their vibratory consciousnesses at the edges of its meaty mind. They were collectives, hundreds of thousands of individual mounds brought together in ropey angulation, who had opened themselves to as much other meat as they could. They pounded the meat field with heavy footfalls, splotching the land with deep indentations, leaving lakes of blood in their wakes, absorbing many of the smaller mounds into themselves. The sight might have made the mound afraid, if it didn't know that all was meat, and that this absorption was merely the way of things in a wholly meat-made world. Still, it avoided these monstrous things intuitively, having no desire to lose that much of itself, although, since all was meat, it wasn't sure why.

After a time the mound became aware of small variations asserting themselves in the topography of the plain, and a slight curvature became apparent to it on the previously flat horizon. The mound shuddered to a stop, formed its thinking appendage, and placed it once again at the bottom of the various vacuities that approximated its face.

Has this curve always been? How have I now just noticed it? Could this mean the end is near?

As usual, the other meat responded.

It does not matter. We must go, it reminded the mound.

Without response, the mound continued.

As it moved further toward the curve it became distracted by the many new attenuations of meat that manifested themselves within— and possibly because of—this incurvation.

Many that had previously shared in its travailing took on a grayish hue, as if being drained of their vitality. They slowed and slowed, and seemed to push against the sharply forward pitch the land was taking. They flailed fruitlessly against this falling, frenzied as if in terror.

Others battled one another in violent crashings, slamming into each other, dashing themselves apart, only to reform commingled. Then, having gained understanding from this violent merging, they undulated together, having moved from one carnal desire to another. The mound could feel the vague impressions their ecstasies left upon the land. It felt a nearly overwhelming desire to join them—to join in—but it ignored these strong temptations and continued to flow and fold itself forward.

Eventually, it came to the end of the curvature, and perceived at its center a vast, black, chasmic maw that swallowed the curve from all around. Ringed around this terrible opening, millions upon millions of other mounds formed a single meat continuum that was slowly emptying itself into the abyss. It could see them entering this continuum and could follow them vaguely after they merged with it. The mound watched as, one by one, they all fell into the awesome fissure.

It tried once again to stop, to think, but by now the force that had always pulled it had joined with the gravity of the Void, and both exerted a firm hold over it.

Here we go, said the other inside meat, and the mound could do nothing but agree.

It tumbled into the continuity, immediately feeling all the other meat at once. This was the apex, a place of meat unburdened, where their collective experience would be processed into the great repository. This is what was always sought, it now knew. Its individuality, had it ever really had any, was drowned by the terrible excitations of this brotherhood, and it happily floated through the experiential dream unabated by any former doubts.

Finally, after what seemed like an eternity, the mound reached the gulf's edge. It felt a wind upon its surface—the first thing that wasn't meat to touch its skin—and considered all it had been through, all it had learned in its time in the world of meat, and when it was done, it braced itself accordingly. Then, it pitched itself inside.

The Man Who Collected Ligotti

The Performer

During the throes of my most recent bout of melancholia I took to walking around the city, several miles per day after work. Truthfully, I can tell you that I took no pleasure in these daily jaunts, as my persistent malady will not allow such things, I merely sought to shorten the length of time between my return home each afternoon from my job at the office, to that time in the evening when I could finally permit myself the luxury of that little death called sleep.

It was on one of these pleasureless strolls that I happened upon a small cafe tucked away at the end of one of the many refuse-filled alleys that have multiplied in number throughout the city in recent years. The signage was plain, and bore only the name "Cafe," and hung over a door so paint-stripped as to be almost bare. I remember thinking to myself that this edifice must assuredly have been for an establishment that would perfectly mirror my pervasive mood.

Upon entering the establishment called simply, "Cafe," I found myself to be completely correct. The scarce tables, with their mismatched chairs, the threadbare and faded couches, the sparse and beleaguered lights and waitstaff, the ramshackle stage at the far end covered over with uneven curtains, the blacked-out windows—all these things gave the impression that I had entered some secret place in my own mind.

I was welcomed by not being welcomed. I found a seat, was ignored by the staff, and left after a suitable amount of time having not spoken to another person at all. But even though I took part in no traditional conversation, there was another kind of conversation happening, one I was definitely a part of, along with the rest of the small congregation gathered that day in "Cafe."

It happened in the spaces between deep sighs, and muffled sobs, in the nervous shuffle of feet, and in the rustle of collars during quick nervous glances. It was a conversation only the loneliest can have, and it was about the same thing lonely people always talk about, whether they mean to or not.

This establishment called "Cafe" became a favorite destination of mine, for in no other place could there be found a larger contingent of people who seemed to share the same malady that afflicts me so tenaciously. The face of every person who haunts the cafe called "Cafe" is an almost perfect match to the one who awaits me every time I make the mistake of looking into a mirror. I suppose it is possible I kept going back because I felt the need for company in my misery, but I suspect I just wanted to be assured that I wasn't the only person in the world who so pervasively didn't care.

So regular became my visits to the cafe that I discovered that every Friday there was held, on the ramshackle stage, a series of performances from the regular patrons of "Cafe." Invariably, on Fridays, at some nebulous time in the evening, one of the patrons would get up from their seat and shuffle their way up to the stage, demarking the beginning of the performances, at which time they would listlessly execute some artistic act of varying quality, before handing the stage off to the next person. And so on, and so forth.

One soul, a man with small, ovoid glasses, has an ancient dummy held over from a long-forgotten age of that much maligned pursuit known as ventriloquism, and he uses this nameless wooden compatriot, with its faded, chipped face, to tell dark limericks that make little to no sense to the ear. One woman warbles funereal songs while shuffling back and forth across the stage with dirty bare feet, and still another merely sits on a stool, vacillating between raucous laughter and uncontrollable sobs.

Each performer who took the ramshackle stage on Fridays, upon finishing their act, looked to me as if the activity gave them some measure of peace, a break in the listless gray storm in which we all reside. Something inside me was stirred by this prospect, and so it was that I came to join these strange performers, reading each Friday the stories of an author I had only recently discovered, and who I have come to understand shares deeply our collective pain.

I found a few of this author's books in boxes in my attic, left behind by a former tenant of my home. So taken was I by the writing therein that I found I had something to look forward to each time my hand passed into a box and found yet another cover bearing his name. Only someone with a profound understanding of the affliction shared by myself and the patrons of "Cafe" could possibly write such bleak and truthful tales. I knew that if I attended the Friday performances carrying one of these books from which to read, that the crowd would appreciate them just as I have, inasmuch as any of us have the capacity to still do such a thing.

So it was that I set about sharing the tales of this forlorn teller, and soon my weeks became nothing but blurs between Fridays at the cafe called "Cafe," which were the only days that now contained any semblance of living to me. When I read, I rarely looked into the crowd, as it was always filled with the same faces, and those faces never betrayed anything more than apathy, so it was easy for me to overlook the presence of the watching man for a considerable amount of time. When I did finally notice him—sitting at my table, his lamp-like eyes reflecting back at me—so unnerved was I that I cut off the story about a man obsessed with a cassette tape, thus depriving my audience of the crucial twist from which the story derives its power.

By the time I'd made my way off the stage and back to my seat, the man was gone. Upon inquiry I was informed by one of the waitstaff that the watching man had been attending my readings for weeks, somehow managing to arrive just in time for my turn on the stage, sitting down at my table, and leaving once I'd finished.

I had no idea what to make of this, so I put it out of my mind lest it aggravate my already worsening condition, and would subsequently forget about the watching man during the blurry week that followed my discovery of him.

But there he was, as if only to remind me, waiting at my table upon the completion of my reading the following Friday.

He rose as I neared the table and doffed the round hat he wore. I mumbled a greeting, asked him what I could do for him. In response, he simply reached into his coat and produced a book bearing the author's name, one I was unfamiliar with. He smiled as I stared at it, agog.

Returning the book to his inside coat pocket, he turned abruptly and made for the cafe door. Upon reaching it, he beckoned me with a swoop of his right hand without looking back, pushed the door open with the cane he held in his left, and walked through.

I could do nothing but follow.

The Paranoiac

There is a man—one of tall and spindly stature, wearing a round hat and brown overcoat, carrying a thin, black cane with a silver cap—who has followed me nearly all my life.

At the start, designs and patterns were his province. I first noticed him as a toddler, lurking in the gauzy, imprisoning mesh of my playpen. His form was unmistakable, and as I traced it with my pudgy, pink fingers over and over, burning his outline into my mind, I learned, inch by inch, to fear him; his meshy eyes staring, his uncaned hand reaching.

So disturbed was I by him that my parents were forced to throw the playpen out, as I could no longer bear to be inside it after. I would scream if they brought me near it, if it was mentioned, if they dared to walk me by the room in which it resided, regardless of a closed door, and when my father took it to the curb to be collected, I stood on the sofa and watched through the front window, just to be sure. When I found it removed the next day, I believed it meant I had escaped him, that I had won.

Unfortunately, this was not so.

The man continued to linger across the years of my childhood. He lurked in scattered shadows, in the patterns of furniture, skulked in the weave of our carpets. He reached down from our water-stained ceiling, out from between the ever-present wrinkles of my clothes, wavered in the pungent, sticky smoke of my father's hand-rolled cigarettes, and hid in the persistent rash beneath my arms. He even roamed the greenish, blackish mold that propagated along the walls of our basement, where my mother would banish me whenever she grew tired of listening to me go on and on.

Outside of our home, he lived in whorls of tree bark, checkered flannel, plumes of spark and ash, in avian murmurations splashed across the sky; reeds of grass, mud puddles, brickwork, piles of garbage, the medium didn't seem to matter, only the message. He was coming, and there was nothing I could do to stop it.

His ever presence resulted in a pervading anxiety, a clinging cloud, whose causal nature produced countless calamities; accidents of distraction, frustrations injurious, and inevitable. Once, I was severely punished for cutting him from the chestnut locks of a classmate, and there he was afterward, purpled in the bruising left behind by my beating, defiant, as if nothing else should have been expected.

But the worst, by far, were those times when I found him cloaked between starbursts tattooed upon the backs of my eyelids, tightly closed in futile attempts to banish him.

There was nowhere where he wasn't.

Over time, as my mind gradually took on a less literal bent, I found my opinion of the man relaxed. After all, he was only an outline in form, not tangible beyond the varying lines that approximated him, and by my teenage years I came to believe that he was at worst a trick of the mind, a leftover trauma, carried over from that first encounter into every one that followed. It became amusing to me that I should have allowed myself to be bedeviled by such a small trick for so great a time. Eventually, I would laugh out loud at the man whenever I saw him, forcing him from my mind's darkest, most fearful places, and into the light of absurd frivolities. In doing so I reduced him, bit by bit, into a joke.

This, he could not abide, and shortly after my fourteenth birthday made this fact abundantly clear by modifying the way he appeared to me, taking shape in full color, with full features, and doing so upon a billboard situated along a stretch of highway navigated by my morning bus to school.

Time slowed the first time I saw him in this new manifestation. His dirt-brown coat whipped behind him. The silver top of his cane gleamed. The urine yellow nails of his reaching hand were cracked, and his eyes were pinpricks glinting from the shadow cast by his hat's wide brim. A wry smile sneered up one side of his face mocking me, as if to say: "How funny am I now, you wrong-headed child?"

The apoplectic fit I had in response to this unvoiced question was an answer in and of itself, for while it contained howls and screams, there was absolutely no laughter in it.

After that, I became a distraction to my fellow students, as the man took to appearing only while I was among them. In class, he would stand in the margins of textbooks, in the background of school flyers, on posters in the hallways, in murals covering their walls. Sometimes, I would walk down a corridor and see him in some fashion only to round a corner and see him again, waiting for me, as if he were walking me to class, which of course he was. And when I would arrive, I would find that, naturally, he had beaten me there, creeping somewhere within my eyeline.

I threw the books he squatted in, tore down the posters, defaced his murals, and soon became a "problem student," expelled for my aberrant behavior. This was his plan, to return me to the isolation of my home, where he could have me all to himself.

My parents, who had little patience for me as it was, were furious, and relegated me, permanently, to the basement of our home, forcing me to finish my education by schooling myself from books they sometimes left at the bottom of the basement stairs, along with my meals.

And of course, in every book, there was the man, sneering in supposed victory.

I came to believe that I was simply insane, paranoid to the point of delusion, the man merely a manifestation of this rampant derangement. He had to be, for the alternative was too much to bear. So I ignored him, refusing to so much as glance at him when he popped around the edges of paragraphs, or profaned an illustration. I treated him much as the eyes do the nose, and by the arrival of my eighteenth birthday, at which time I found myself unceremoniously ejected from my childhood home, I'd tricked myself into believing he did not exist.

I became a derelict, thrown atop the tangled pile of other browned and ragged leavings that increasingly choked the streets of our town. I became another of the specters ignored by those still blessed to travel between their daily distractions. And in one of the hunched and faded edifices that grow like fungus across our formerly fair city, those places abandoned and no longer populated by the distracted, one in which I and many others of my new ken had come to find shelter, he found me.

And I found him, changed again.

As I had graduated to adulthood, transformed from homed to unhomed, he had graduated as well, from the second dimension to the third, transformed himself into a tangible, touchable being, leaned up against the far interior wall of the moldy building inside of which I'd come to lay my head by night.

He looked at me across a sea of other derelicts, propped on his cane, reaching, and over a din of moans and sobs I heard with my ears, for the first time, his voice; soft and colored with rasp. And what he said was the very thing I'd always imagined him saying, the whisper that infected me so long ago with his presence.

He said, "I am coming."

And then, he pushed off that interior wall of that inferior home, stepped carefully across the rotten floor, between the rotten things that populated it, and came for me.

And for the first time in my life, he was welcomed.

The Dreamer

Silent liquidity, formless smoke and ephemera; a coalescence each night as I lay my head upon my pillow, the result of which is a locality that can only exist in the darkest of dreamscapes.

It smells of must and rot, has rows and corridors filled with shelves bursting with faded impressions, is populated by broken machines and gadgets, puppets, dummies, dolls, and mannikins, all of them crammed between books teeming with lost antiquity.

I have walked it up and down, climbed ladders interminable into heights of darkness unyielding, and I have never found an end. Such is the way of dream places, and if this dream place were like other dream places I would not deign to speak of it, but this dream place is more real than those others, lit not just by sputtering, unseen candles, but with a definite sureness of being. This place exists. It is out there, somewhere, and I believe that I am close to being swallowed up, digested by it, my fate to be filed onto one of its endless shelves, collected amongst its trappings.

I know it to be a place for the lost, the weak and the wounded. For you see, I myself am lost, I am weak, I have been wounded. I remain so. This place knows this. It sought me out, as it seeks out all things irreparable, feeds upon them, sucks them dry of their cracks and sharp edges, until they are nothing more than twisted, soft curves fading into entropy.

Its shelves are covered in strange dust, which yields not to the touch. Its floors are layered with dirt and grime that sticks to the sole. Its ladders are filled with cracks, and crawl with woodlice, making each step up an exercise in fateful temptation. Though they never break, the fear that they will persists, and this fear nourishes it. It hungers for this fear just as much as it does despair, as it does loneliness. It drains and drains, bloats itself upon those most hateful of emotions, reducing the collected into ultimate stillness.

It has a strong, deterministic will, which it wields with careful discrimination, and along with this will it also bears a face, a face with eyes that watched you, a nose that sniffed you out, ears that heard your cries. This face rests upon a head, one that decided upon you, wished to bring you to it, and this head rests upon shoulders that carried you, arms that deposited you. It has legs and feet as well, ones that walked away immediately after.

In aggregate, a man.

You see, there is a proprietor of this place, felt, but unseen. Seen or not, however, he lingers there, his ubiety leaving an impression upon every inch of the space. He can be felt upon the pages of the books I try to peruse, but can never read. He can be smelt in the red fungal bloom bursting from their pages. He can be heard in echoed footsteps that seem to be, but cannot be, my own. When I climb the ladders, he is there behind me, but should I look to catch him climbing, only wisps of smoke-like darkness waft between the rungs. He rests in the dull glinting of the broken machines, in the whine of the dead gadgets as they fruitlessly struggle to come to life. He is in the dead, lifeless eyes of the dolls and the dummies, in the featureless facades of the broken mannikins.

He is there, but not there. He permeates.

I wish I could know this proprietor. I have called out so many times to him, rushed up and down the corridors professing this very wish, shaken the bookcases and ladders in sorrowful fury. But as I said, he does not answer. He merely brings me time and again to his dreamplace, taking slowly from me my darkness.

He does not wish to know me, I think, for I suppose I am to him as unimportant as any other thing he has collected for depletion. He only wishes to know the things inside of me that nourish him.

He probably believes that I am angry. He no doubt thinks that

I wish to attack him in some way, even though to do so would be the height of futility, I'm sure. Maybe he thinks that I would beg for freedom from the fate he has visited upon me. Perhaps he believes that I will ask to join him, to assist him in his efforts in some way, as if I could ever do the things he does. I'm positive that of the multitudes who have come before me, all of them, in some fashion, have desired to interact with this man, but I doubt few if any of them sought the thing that I seek.

I wish for only one thing. I wish to offer him my sincere, and profound gratitude.

I spent my last evening in his dreamplace screaming this intention into the infinite. I told of all the hurtful things from which he is delivering me. I wept in appreciation of his efforts, held my hands above me in supplication, before tearing at my skin to offer that pain to him as well. I even made a space upon the shelves and climbed inside, curling myself into a ball, to show him just how natural I would find my eventual placement within his menagerie.

While he did not answer me directly, there was something, a slight touch upon my shoulder, no more than a whisper; there but for a moment, and then gone as quickly as it came. Afterward, I believe I heard soft footsteps moving away from me, and a click upon the wood floor accompanying them, like that of a cane. I am sure that he was with me, that I reached out to him and he briefly grabbed hold.

I believe my time is nigh.

Tonight, I return there, to show him again how much I desire his gift of consummation.

I lay my head upon my pillow. I close my eyes.

He is here.

The Collector

You spoke to me, sir, and I have listened. The lessons you imparted have not been in vain, for I have taken your wisdom and transformed it into action. You uncovered the truth of it—that gnawing, brooding, laughing, terrible thing behind every other thing—and you brought that knowledge to the world, tried to educate these fools. And how did they reward your good will? They all but ignored you.

But I did not.

I could find but one flaw in your design, and that flaw is that you delivered your wisdom to them, hoping that they would use it. I wouldn't have thought you to be such an optimist. No, these troglodytes would never, could never, do what needs to be done. They are caught up in the ruse, the trick, the "conspiracy." They are lost in the dream.

But I am awake, and when I am done with my work, my own "special plan," I will bring the Void to us.

I was first and foremost a seller and keeper of books; a collector, purveyor of things mysterious, and esoteric, and it was during the course of this perveyance that I stumbled upon your work.

Outside of this vocation, I was also a hobbyist, a fellow writer in fact, and it was this hobby that allowed me to understand the true nature of a writer. We—if you'll forgive the vulgar comparison of you and I—are conduits, prisms through which other, more strange truths and realities are projected. Only through us, and those like us, can certain things take shape in the world of humanity. Religions and the sciences, those idiocies that can only hope to do what we do, could never comprehend the truth or value of that which is our providence. We purposefully do what they do only by accident. We make the unreal, real. Not that I have to tell you that, of course, but it is important to me that you know that I know it, so that you'll see that I am in full possession of the facts, that I am not doing what I'm doing out of anything other than complete knowledge and understanding.

Esoterica, by its very nature, begets all manner of odd illuminations, so you can imagine that beyond the realms of academic and artistic literature lie whole continents of fantastic and even supernatural discourse, representing themselves not as fiction, but as actual fact, and in my efforts to aggregate the various knowledges I spent so many of my years meticulously gathering, I became frustrated, for there seemed no way for me to join it together into anything that could come close to sense. I could feel the truth in my bones, could see the puzzle depicting it laid out in pieces before me, but could not conceive of how to arrange them. I am not too proud to admit that, in the end, I reached the edge of complete madness trying to find that unifying thing that would make it all coagulate. And then, your work arrived on my doorstep, and pulled me back from the brink.

I became obsessed with it from my very first foray. I could see your vision immediately, and with each new tale I would dash back and forth between the shelves of my shop, corroborating and validating that which you so clearly defined. It was as if you put a key into the locked door that had been keeping my enlightenment at bay, and when the inky truth came flooding out, I was overtaken by the mania that followed.

I instructed every contact I'd accrued during my time as a book-keeper to find and deliver to me anything you'd ever written. "If this man's name is on it, I want it" was the directive, and within a month I had it all in my possession. I consumed it, ravenously, my head not touching a pillow for days, until every word was transferred from the pages into my head.

Next, I made a great collage across the back wall in my back room, blasphemously tearing out pages and affixing them to it, pairing them with other pages from other books that validated their philosophies and assertions. My basic needs were ignored, nearly outright. That I was required to leave the room to relieve myself became the height of annoyance, and if my idiotic vanity had not prevented it, I may have done so right there, if only to not waste a single, precious moment in the pursuit of that which I could sense was just out of reach.

Then, it was finished. Standing before it I trembled, and as it slowly imparted upon me its great revelation, I collapsed into a ball of exultation and exhaustion. With your help, I had completed that which I'd been pursuing unknowingly my entire life: A fully formulated, and perfect, plan.

It was so simple. All I needed to do was what you had done so many times, what all writers do. I needed to conjure that which is unreal, bring it to life, and then do what I do best: collect it.

You see, the very essence of that which you dubbed "The Tsalal," and what I refer to simply as the Void, as you well know, stands behind and is incorporated into everything you've ever written. You saw past the illusion and stared into its eye. You beheld its shadow, and then cast that shadow upon each and every one of the little mirrors of yourself you "created" and called characters, imbuing them with a piece of that essence. Unfortunately, there was no way for me to collect that essence from those little yous, as they are too far removed from myself—and my own creative vision—to be of use.

But, there was another way.

I realized that all I needed to do was create my own Tiny Toms, ones I felt most strongly represented you. Much as you did, I would cast upon them the shadow of truth, and then—through various alchemical and arcane practices gleaned from my collection—force them out of the world of the unreal and into the world of the real to suffer in the ways in which you have suffered, and once that suffering hardened them into diamond like prisms, I would find and collect these tulpas in turn—The Performer, The Paranoiac, and The Dreamer—drawing from them that essence, and distilling it into a singular form, made up of only it.

Sadly, they were not enough. These homunculi were insufficient on their own. My talent and imagination proved inadequate. The thing I made from them was half-formed, embryonic, slithering in the pool in which I keep it, moaning and babbling incoherence, incapable of what I needed it to do. It required something *more*.

I puzzled over this for some time. How could I extract that which I needed if I could not use your characters, or my own? Truly, a frustrating conundrum. Then, one night—while stroking my malformed avatar as it warbled—I found myself engaging a book of interviews you'd given, hoping to glean some heretofore unrealized answer from your wisdom. And then, between the coos and the gurgles of my creation, it came to me.

I realized that I needed to collect a different sort of distillation. It occurred to me that not only do your characters carry the required essence, but also the readers and acolytes of the work you created by showing their struggles to the world. I was but one prism through which your vision was refracted. Your influence, niche though it may be, has created so many more prisms, equal to or even greater than my own.

So I went about collecting the most afflicted of your followers; the monk, the musician, the German, the academic, the journalist, and finally, the puppeteer. I drained them, one by one, of you; fed their distillate to my mewling abomination.

It was nearly enough. As you can plainly see, it is now almost fully formed, glutted on their contributions. But yet, still incomplete.

There is but one thing left to do.

None of them could reach the required purity. The essences I gleaned from them were too cloudy, too infected with the lie. To bring about the end of all this nonsense, my phylactery requires a refinement that can only be found in a singular person.

And now, here we are.

It was the puppeteer who led me to you, but do not blame him, he did not do so willingly. I tore the information from him before taking the rest of what I needed. He begged me to spare you. I couldn't make him understand.

As I did with him, I've tried tonight to make you see what's necessary, to accept it. This is the only way, you must believe me. Search your feelings, you know it to be true. For *my* work to be done, for *my* special plan to be enacted, I must fit this final piece. Look down there, into that pool at your feet, at that thing which has started to resemble you. Behold the labyrinthine blackness swarming behind its eyes, ready to burst out and consume us all. Be honest, don't you find it beautiful?

I suppose it doesn't matter.

I won't lie, it will hurt. It must. For what it's worth, I am genuinely sorry you will never get to see the thing our creation brings about when it finally howls its summoning and pulls your "Tsalal," my Void, screaming into the world. Don't you worry, though. I will greet it for the both of us.

Are you ready?

No?

Let's begin anyway.

Welcome, dear Tom, to The End.

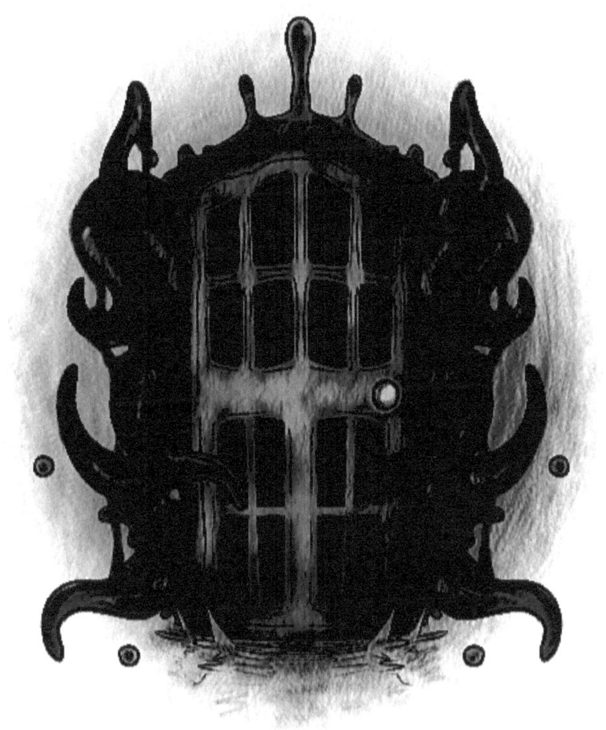

THE BLACK

Demodorum

In the gray wastes that lay between death and the waiting Void, deep beneath the necropolis of Dessecai, on a profane altar, The Whispering Book, Demodorum, lies.

Held open and fast by The Reader, his moldering eyes locked on its pages, Demodorum is attended by servants called by its whispers; falsely pious men, whose hearts in life held no belief, finding false redemption now in Demodorum. They clawed their way down through the decayed earth to come and fall prostrate before it, mistaking its murmuring for benediction. Piled high, they writhe upon one another, wheezing prayers to match the book's endless gibbering; a mass of choral carrion.

Far above sprawls Dessecai, creation of Demodorum and bastion of the wandering dead. Those who find themselves in this land are lost, bound to the life they knew, and hazily afraid of the infinite fathoms for which they are destined. The gray gives them cold, familiar meat to house their transient souls, and they bring these husks with them to Dessecai.

At first they are afflicted by the surroundings, no words leaving their rotted lips, no cries issuing from shredded throats—too awful is the truth for shriveled brains to bear. Demodorum hears their silent suffering, and gladly takes the load. It first whispered the city to life in order to give the woeful quarter, and keeps the city standing to spite the hungry Void.

The Void, originator and devourer of all existence, that place that is not a place, where ideas are formed, defecated into being, only to be abandoned upon birth; the ultimate source and destination of all moving parts in the grand machine, who, once untethered, will always find their way back. Now not always, determines Demodorum as it herds all arrivals to the gray toward its spiteful creation. *Come,* says the book in what services for their minds, *find your way to Dessecai.* And they do.

At the gates they are met, these vestiges of life, by more of Demodorum's sweet whispers, floating up from beneath and promising them paradise—lazy summer days, calm, restful nights, love and hope, green grass and warm rain. *In Dessecai all can be as it was,* promises the book, *submit and be happy. Stay and be free.*

Any who would deny this lure are cast away, doomed to float the desolate wastes until such time as they are swallowed back into eternity. Doubt never lies dormant in Dessecai; its vaporous fingers too easily clutch at the dreamers and the dreamed. Doubt is anathema to magic, never to be allowed. Demodorum snuffs it, within or without, placing visions of skinless torment into the minds of doubters, sending them howling back into the gray, never to again gaze upon great Dessecai.

Those who submit, however, are gifted visions of crystallized life. Demodorum provides for them salvation tucked away in pockets of perfection. Gossamer cages of memory keep the contented dead. *No dark eternity could ever reach you here,* it tells them, *the walls of Dessecai are both thick and high, never to be breached.*

So they go about in a fictitious normal, assured of their safety, and mingle with each other in a shuffling semblance of living. Passing by but not quite seeing, never glimpsing into others' dreams; walking imaginary pets, eating imaginary meals, seeking pleasures simple and complex, and fulfilling them in blasphemous mockeries only possible in Dessecai, the truth of their putrid world hidden by Demodorum's mercy.

To preserve them it must deceive, must proffer lies to keep insanity, and the Void's promise of dark infinity at bay.

Demodorum hates the infinite Void, maternal nemesis of reality. No cohesion possible in that pit of everything, imagination nonexistent where no stories can be told. Books are story keepers, after all, and Demodorum is no different. Unlike other books, however, Demodorum can create. Defiant on its altar, the book wields a formidable will in the war against the infinite, Dessecai an ever-growing monument to its frequent victories.

Being nothing and everything at once, the Void is, as much as it is anything, indifferent to this conflict, and this greatly angers Demodorum; the unnoticing existence of its creator as hateful in its mind as in that of any other learned, living thing.

Before Dessecai, Demodorum spent the first eons of its existence screaming, sending cries into the darkness and receiving no reply—no answers offered, no wisdom gained. Only despair had Demodorum until it ceased its wailing, and surrendered to despondency. Then, it heard the dead. Then, it found its purpose.

The first of its whispers drew the supplicants, detestable apostates who came and laid bare for it the weakness of man. They had believed in nothing, sure they would return to it once gone. Demodorum stood deific before them in defiance of that belief. They chose one among them to open the book, thinking themselves liberators, and so The Reader came to gaze upon the pages. Struck dumb by the majesty of

Demodorum freed, he never again addressed the congregation, his mind and theirs instantly melting into pools of faith.

Finding freedom, Demodorum reached out, sending its consciousness spreading across the gray, looking for more than death. Only the Void awaited. The scope of it staggered the book; the sheer immensity of that folding forever teaching to it awe—the ecstasy of nothingness eternal teaching to it want. The sorcery of the gray enraptured Demodorum, and alike the rest of the restless it yearned to make its way back into the unending deeps.

Tragically, this was not to be.

Demodorum is an abstract, an anomaly of creation. Wrung out of lunacy and spat out by the Void, its unique existence marks it as the only truly living thing within the gray. In abhorrence of a vacuum, the book was conceived by the universe and projected from its progenitor's derangement; left abandoned and alone to find its way.

The book is required to maintain the crucial balance, as such it must exist to offer choice; its role not to return to the Void, but to try to turn any who would do so against the notion entirely. It stands anomalous because, among the living, Demodorum has no choice. There will be no absolution, no peace of not existing. In perhaps the greatest tragedy of all, Demodorum is eternal.

Cruelly, it was unaware of these things. Its definitions are defined by the dead to which it calls, its perceptions shaped by their fleeting memories.

So it gathered them, filling the cavernous halls of its resting place with abundant disciples, seeking knowledge from the remnants of their minds. It learned nothing but dogma from their ceaseless prayers; of gods, of faith, of the ironic inconsistencies across all of man's guesswork, the information only helpful in strengthening its ability to hold the flock together.

It was not a god, surmised the book, for a god would not be so impotent. It could issue no commands. Those that heard it were always given choice, their willingness to obey based solely on the degree of their desires. The supplicants wanted nothing but to worship, their thoughts completely glutted on Demodorum's "glory." It found them easy to gather and keep. They were many, but their number proved a pittance compared to the wealth of dead left wandering. It needed more than what the adherent horde could provide.

Thus, it envisioned Dessecai. Not at first to keep the dead, only to gather them briefly, to offer temporary respite and learn of the living world of which it was not. From the first billion who passed through, the book learned everything it needed. Expectation, hope, fear. Resentment, anger, rage. It became fueled by hatred born from abandonment, stoked by a consistently spurned belief in eventual deliverance. After that, it kept all the dead it could, hoping that an act of defiance would force a remonstration, an *acknowledgement*, not knowing that like any other living thing, it served exactly as intended.

For millennia it watched them, like fishes in a tank, delighting in the peace it afforded. Intensely focused was Demodorum on making their conjured sheens of life as palatable as possible. It felt a kinship with them, after all, as equally wronged by the Void were they, it believed. Protector, it fashioned itself, its hatred gradually dissipating into arrogance. It would one day be equal to the Void and keep all the dead from it. It would defeat its great foe and reign as benevolent ruler. Fancy discovered Demodorum as it dreamed of eventual triumph.

Then came to it a reckoning.

So simple was the endeavor Demodorum did not foresee its limits. When its whispers became weakened by the size of its first brood, it did not perceive it. The walls crumbled, the streets cracked, and doubt crept in where it was not looking and the spell frayed quickly before cascading into complete collapse. Dessecai's dead were lost, taken by the gluttonous Void.

Shocked was Demodorum at its powerlessness, to see such merry made of its war. Finding itself humbled, the book remained undaunted, for among the myriad things it learned from those it kept, tactics were among them. It recalled battles lost, but wars not over, shrouded revenges sought and gained. Broadening its enmity to include the legions that abandoned it—as did the Void so long ago—it reaffirmed its purpose in keeping the ungrateful dead. And to those who followed after in the streets of Dessecai, Demodorum would bring misery. This, it vowed.

To prepare for this undertaking the book turned its thoughts inward, seeking an introspective bent on which to hang its vengeful inclinations. What it discovered once inside itself astounded. A portion of the dead thought lost were waiting, their spirits having fled from the collapse not to the Void, but somehow deeper within the dream, into Demodorum's chronicled thoughts. A memorial ghost of Dessecai existed there, and the dead most fearful of The Void now desperately gripped at that glimmer rather than return to the yawning dark. Bound were they now to the everlasting pages, their stories intertwined with its own. No longer were they merely distracted, but wholly consumed, fates sealed by their final choice.

Demodorum knew delight. Its rage assuaged by relief, it turned its full attention on those pitiful refugees, all seized by madness absent its whispers. It cradled and soothed, rocking them gently back into complacency, painstakingly recreating their halcyon cages one by one. Now that they were firmly nestled, existing solely in its bosom, Demodorum felt answerable for any woe that might befall them. Its steel resolve manifolded in the face of this responsibility. Now, it *was* a god.

Taken by inspiration begat by newfound divinity, the book devised a devious stratagem. It would rebuild its necrotic net and cast it wide, trawling the gray for floundering spirits, bringing them home to the safety of its new cistern. Two versions of Dessecai would exist from now on, the trap above and the tank below. This pleased Demodorum, and the giddy satisfaction it felt from this endeavor slaked its hunger for meaning for ages. Contentment reigned, and its rule was fair and good.

Inevitably, the tank below became an insufficient vessel in which to hold the soulful bloat, and in answering this dilemma Demodorum discovered yet another delightful hobby. It built within itself a world. A demi-plane was constructed to the specifications of its legions' demands, inspired by colorful musings and painted with mercurial desire. Their souls split from the shambling cadavers provided by the gray, the dead in this new kingdom were returned to warm bodies and functioning cognizance. Their wants were plenty and ever changing; abundant visions did Demodorum create to satiate their ceaseless yearnings. Yet the more it gave them, the less satisfied they became.

While potent, the magic held by Demodorum was not as powerful as that of the gray. As a result, the subsumed spirits, having regained their senses, began slowly to understand the state in which they now persisted. Their minds revolted in the face of millenia, rejected the shimmering dreamscapes gifted them, and degraded into despair. To test the limits of the unending existence they now shared, a number began purposefully to throw themselves at danger, hoping to bring death. None of them found it. The new forms that housed them could not feel pain, could not be harmed, but their psyches suffered profusely. The swiftly purveying sadness infecting its new macrocosm alarmed and angered Demodorum, but the book would not be so easily bested. Its conviction only amplified.

It wrought for them the Pleasure Fields of Zom, and the tranquil waters of Brightwick Bay, erected the pillowed Tower of Xevosh, and the prim, delicate minarets of Anthromor, City of Dazzling Lights, assembled, branch by branch, the elfish domain of Condoroaca, and composed the hypnotic music that swayed through the bowered avenues there. From the walls of sweet-smelling Hyphrovai to the lush, poetic gardens of Alurra, Demodorum's vast and varied vistas were as grand and epic in scope as they were useless to the task it had set itself. None of it mattered to the increasingly despondent dead, and they castigated the illusory heavens in their sorrow.

Release, they cried in unison, and only release would bring them peace. No adventure could supplant their wish for extrication. Ranging the sheer, sea-sprinkled cliffs of Dovaru answered not the maddening epochs that lay before them. The phantasmagoric dance of the wildlife that scampered in the groves of Bothlovere, settled no accounts for any among the throngs who witnessed. Deep and abiding became their anguish until the book could ignore it no more. They flung themselves from the bluffs of Dovaru and aggravated the animate creatures in the Bothloverian brakes, hoping to be gored or mauled for their efforts. A longing for the relief that had once been promised by the Void became most desirous to those who remembered it, and those who remembered it were all.

It was this persistent wishing that finally broke the book. Furious, it brought to them destruction to match its rampant creation, attempting to bring reason with ruin. It removed the protective charms that had been keeping harm at bay, and let loose the long-forgotten sensation known once to them as pain. It rose the tides of Qua'athul to wash away majestic Dim Dalal. The fiery mountain it brought down upon the denizens of Lucadun left the sands beneath a glassy waste that writhed with immolation. It unleashed hordes of steel-bearing barbarians to raze the festooned corridors of sleepy Rocatut, and those arterial thoroughfares thereafter ran with blood. It could not destroy them, like itself they were now eternal, any damage received healing over time, no matter how grievous the wounds. These warnings were intended only to incite them to obedience, to show deference to Demodorum's merciful gifts. The warned moaned only for redemption, and pleaded ever louder to the infinite enemy for reprieve.

Enraged, the book escalated its war exponentially. The boundless imagination it leached from those it trapped could spin wonders both of whimsy and wicked barbarity. Constrained not by the conventional rules of reality, it seeded the lands with aberrations that could only be authored by a being such as it, and visited unique terrors upon the peoples of its pocket dimension. Anti-gravitory monsters plucked victims from the holes in which they hid, and carried them off to charnel nests to be feasted on by maggoty young. The Pleasure Fields were infected, the meadows withered as the spoiled ground trans-formed from soil and rocks to living flesh and bone. One unlucky soul was chosen by Demodorum and grown to obscene size, his body contorted ghoulishly to supplant those swaths of country, and whom-ever trod thenceforth within the newly christened Fleshlands travailed the surface of his warped and twisted skin.

These delightful deviations pleased Demodorum, and soon this hate-fueled furor became its favored fascination.

The more vociferous the spirits were in their regret at the choice to live inside it, that much more vile became the retributions of the tome. Its rising hatred of the thankless masses focused now not just on their ingratitude, but also on their rejection of the gift offered by the Void. As much hatred as it still bore for its enduring nemesis, Demodorum could not deny that the lure of that disentegratory embrace still raised within temptation. Equilibrium comes with understanding, and the fact that these former mortals were offered choice in contrast to its choicelessness filled it with seething bitterness. How dare they reject the only thing it truly wanted? What manner of creatures were they to deny so great an offering? Their arrogance made them worthy of every gruesome revenge. The favor they discarded so freely, became yet another weapon used to mete out its terrible will.

From constant excruciation was borne the utter abandonment of hope, as such, some great pains had been neglected. Dashed faith and mounting dread did not exist when torment was both endless and expected, and it was these sweet sufferings the book grew to covet the use of most. Moderation practiced Demodorum as it eased its molestations and allowed for periods of peace. In what safe spaces could be found, the tortured gathered, and the lamplight of their fear was turned to what lay beyond the walls of those choice necropoli.

It implanted hopeful rumors in their desperate minds, murmurs and legends of escape. It sent them roaming to every corner of its perdition in search of innumerable inexorable inevitabilities. *There is a door beneath the cranial mound of Fachedunn, in the Fleshlands, that leads to the land of the living!*, they hear, and thrust themselves eagerly toward fetidly cavernous defeat. *In noxious Hyphrovai, where skinned dervishes tumble in the lunatic skies, rests a portal that leads to the abyss beyond!*, is the gossip in the streets of Jai-Un-Shoi, and any hopeful rangers who heed this enticement are invariably joined with the flayed cavorters in the Hyphrovaiin air. Countless crushing devastations distributed daily, and in this miserable avocation Demodorum found its peace.

Curious found the book the variance of effect its ministrations had on the aggrieved. Multitudinous remained the huddled masses to be sure, but among them rose another host, one that came to revel in dark perversions. Many were the reasons each soul had feared the Void upon their end, and almost equal in number to mournful graspers were panicked libertines. These latter souls, steel-eyed predators in the living world, began to introduce their own brand of wickedness into the tremulous strongholds where Demodorum's whispers were most subtle.

With abandon did they ravage as they stalked their ever-living victims, and their joyful butchery gratified the malignant tome. Into every precise dissection, every evisceration, through each inch of distended bowel, was woven the book's prideful encouragement.

These slavering hellions traded with it inspiration, their bloodlust and savagery sometimes surprising even Demodorum, inspiring it to deepened malice. While razored mazes and storms of sharpened glass certainly were fantastic, there was beauty to be found in the simplicity of bludgeoned thumbs and burbling throats laced with ruby claret.

Without prompting, they began to twist themselves perversely. Self-mutilation became a favored pastime. Some lashed themselves together through atrocious surgeries and transformed into mockeries of their former humanity. Quadrupedal monstrosities with filed teeth and keen lunacy lumbered through the ashen courts of Condoroaca, and the devilry they brought there pleased the book uniquely.

Some decorated themselves with trophies taken from their victims, sewing to their bodies numerous, flaccid appendages that jostled grotesquely as they bounded upon prey. *Delightful!*, declared Demodorum. As the mottled murderers played, these unforeseen inhumans filled it with bastardized love. With these vile creatures the book found brotherhood and named them The Begotten.

Converse to those abominations were beatific fanatics who found tranquility in suffering. The temporal insanity inflicted upon them deformed them into cultists of false gods conceived within the swells of throbbing throes. They held masses in the open fields of crumbling Allura in order to lure insectoid monsters from their burrows. Willing sacraments they desired to be, seeking penitence in the thrust of mandibular consequence.

Screaming in guttural tongues they danced through the jagged ruins of haunted Anthromor where spectral behemoths surged through their numbers and obliterated their bodies in a cacophony of leviathan bellows. Reconstituting puddles of gore they became, and with newly reformed mouths were made heaps of viscera mewling with adulation.

After every terrible fate, they reveled ever louder. They lauded their myriad imagined gods for this torture, but only Demodorum heard these recognitions. In this twisted form of worship it was fulfilled, and it named these mad zealots The Sanguinists.

A fantastic spectrum of horrors blossomed in the garden of the book's loathing, and it cultivated and named every new species lovingly while basking in the vibrance of each implausible grotesquerie.

So it went, and so it goes. The book and its lamentable progeny finding progressively more obscene delectations in their shared damnation, engaged together in indecency while wrapped warmly in the wafting wails of those who continue to confound conformity. Every facet and rhomboid sparkle of their debauchery is reflected in countless quivering eyes filled with tears shed for reasons as multifarious as the tortures that inspire them. The very air they think they breathe hangs with the acridity of Demodorum's hate, and their crying throats are choked with its condemnations.

No longer merely a tank, the realm of Dessecai is now a perfect wonder of creation, a symphonic atrocity that serves as mirror to the Void that lies beyond. This antithesis of chaotic peace is a clockwork catechism contorting and measuring the breadth of living suffering; a rumbling engine inside an unfortunate vessel drifting upon rancorous waters tainted by melancholic grief. Fit snugly, Demodorum and the fruits of its labor turn now as precisely as all cogs are meant to do within the grand machine, and the universe feasts upon their misery.

Sitting astride its sacrilegious throne, casting unhallowed light on a jabbering throng, the book rides out eternity in the hands of its ill-fated Reader. The apostolic howls of the squirming supplicants mix with its whispers as they carry up through the ground unto the surface of the gray. There it trolls for new recruits among the rambling, and papers their numbers with honeyed invitations to the doom that waits within the jaws of its traps above, and below.

Unknown to the book, however, all who hear that calling have also heard another faint refrain.

Just before stepping through the wall of death, before beginning the journey toward their final choice, every soul is told of the danger. A creeping doubt is laid deep in their thoughts, giving them some chance against the book's sweet, pretending things. This missive relates the tragedy of the tome and its children, warning all of the never-ending stories they will suffer should they dare to turn from naught. The infinite sends this final gambit before surrendering each soul to their fate, and the message that hums in their dying minds begins:

In the gray wastes that lay between death and the waiting Void, deep beneath the necropolis of Dessecai, on a profane altar, The Whispering Book, Demodorum, lies.

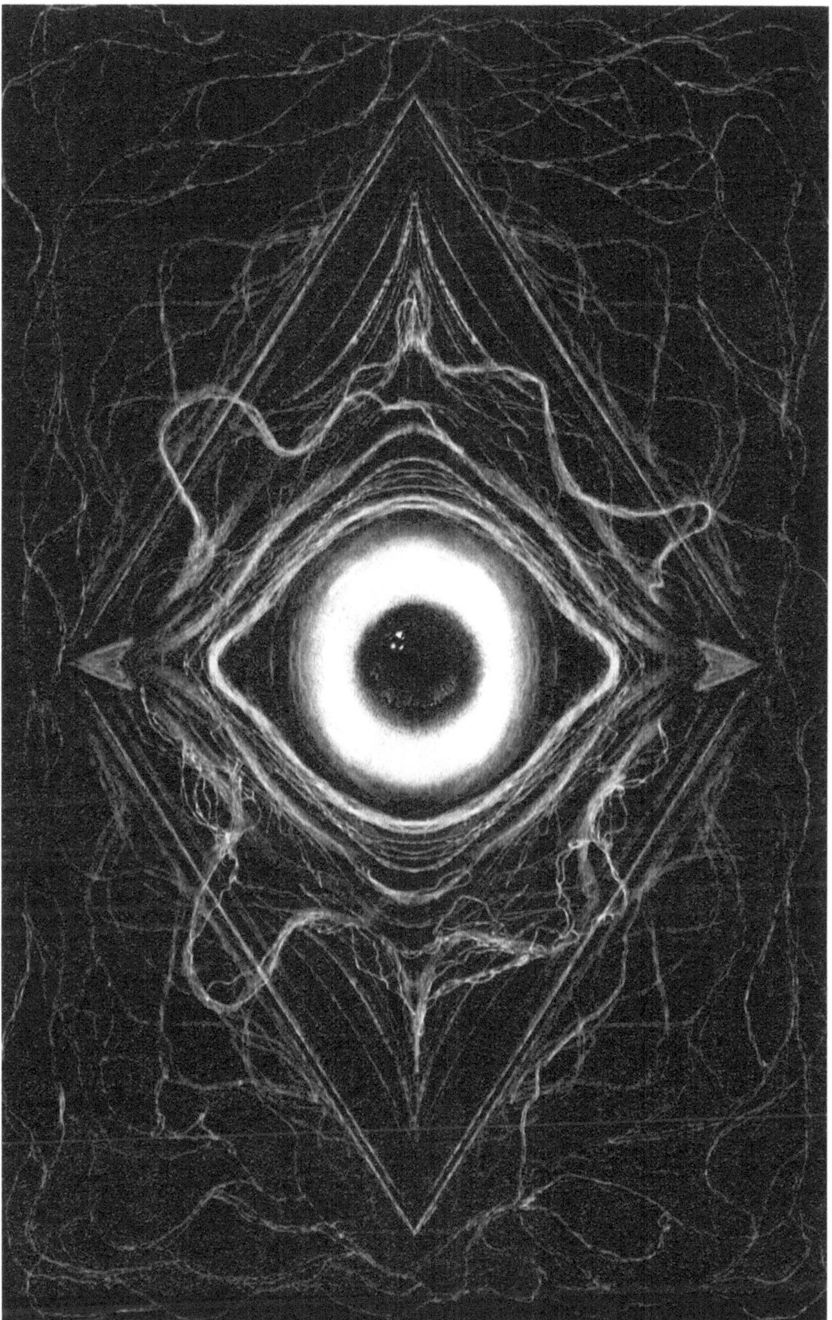

Publication History

"Straw World" was first published in *Vastarien* vol. 5, issue 1

"Knocks" was first published in *Cosmic Horror Monthly* #26

"Little Dirt Boy" was first published in *Tales of Sley House* 2021

"We Must Be Rabbits" was first published in *Cosmic Horror Monthly* #44

"The Success of Dover's Glen: A Study in Four People" was first published in *Chthonic Matter Quarterly*, Spring 2025

"Station 42" was first published in *Collage Macabre: an Exhibition of Art Horror*

"Timmy Thomerson's Turn" was first published in *Night Terrors* vol. 18

"The Face Dealer" was first published in *Dream of Shadows* issue 3

"The Last Case of Dr. Jonah Wexley Abbott" was first published in *Cosmic Horror Monthly* #11

"On the Night Bus" was first published in *Cosmic Horror Monthly* #34

"Something's Off About Wizzle" is original to this collection

"Where We Are, Where We Were, and Where We Will Always Be" was first published in *between doorways: explorations into liminal space*

"In Carnality" was first published in *Lovecraftiana*, vol. 7, issue 5

"The Man Who Collected Ligotti" was first published in *Cosmic Horror Monthly* #49

"Demodorum" was first published in *Cosmic Horror Monthly* #19

Acknowledgements

It goes without saying (although I'm going to say it anyway) that every writer has a long, long road to get to the point where they are putting together this section of their first book. Along the way there are dozens upon dozens, maybe even hundreds of people that have shaped them on that journey, and every one has most assuredly had the same problem as I'm having right now: Not wanting to leave anyone out. Even though that's the goal, I'm almost positive that after finishing they inevitably look back over it long after the fact and remember a name that belongs there, but isn't. I'm sure I'll do the same. Bearing that in mind, I've tried my best to include everyone, and heartfelt apologies to the ones I may have missed.

First I'd like to thank my editor, TJ Price. Now, saying editor is a huge misnomer, considering how much TJ has done to bring this book to life. He positively willed it into being by proposing it in the first place, finding it a home, helping with the title, editing it, helping with putting together the internal format, doing social media graphics, doing typography for the cover, giving constant encouragement, and so much more. Without him this book wouldn't exist, that's a fact, and for that I will be forever grateful. He's a true blue friend.

Speaking of true blue friends, I can't think of a truer, bluer one than Carson Winter. Carson has been there with me nearly my whole writing journey, and I don't think I could have done it without him. He has been a constant source of inspiration, advice, hard truths, support, amusement, and above all, friendship. He is my brother, plain and simple.

When I first started writing seriously, I had no idea what I was doing, and for almost a year I was all on my own, without any peers. I almost gave up, then I found Discord, and the HOWL Society, and everything was right with the world. Particularly, I would like to recognize and thank Richard Snowden-Leak, Timaeus Bloom, Ivy Grimes, Christi Nogle, Patrick Barb, Ai Jiang, P.L. McMillan, Chris O'Halloran (you handsome cad), Alex Wolfgang, the early HOWLers, the WHADSers, and the many, many other people who helped me become a better writer, and person.

Also I would like to take time to thank the many publishers who have helped make my dreams come true, specifically Charles Tyra of *Cosmic Horror Monthly*, who was the first person to buy one of my stories, and has bought so many others, and Jon Padgett, a genuinely kind, and thoughtful human being, not to mention a brilliant writer and editor who is the captain of one of my favorite publishing ventures, Grimscribe Press. You guys are the best.

I'd also like to extend thanks to several people who won't see this, yet deserve to be mentioned regardless. To Helen Hoke for believing that there were kids out there like me who would appreciate what you were gifting us, thank you for the trust. To Thomas Ligotti, thank you for telling the truth, for suffering, and for being an inspiration. To Stephen King, thank you for being my first guiding star. To Robert

Bloch, thanks for the sense of humor, and immaculate timing. To Rod Serling thank you for your bravery, and belief in the good of humanity. To Clark Ashton Smith, thank you for showing me it could be done, and exactly how to do it. And to Jim Steinman, thank you for going over the top and showing me what was on the other side.

I'd also like to thank those people closest to me and my heart. To my parents, Carla and Tony Starr, I want to say thank you for loving me, supporting me always, and never taking away my books. To my children, Kyle, Willow, and Angel, thank you for being the best kids a father could ever ask for, and for being yourselves in spite of me. To my friends Josh, and Rachel for being there so long, listening to me dream about this and always believing I could do it. And to my grandmothers, Gertie and Barbara, both passed, thank you for loving me into being, and saving me when I was drowning.

And last, but certainly not least, I want to thank my wife, Noel. Without you I would have nothing. Without you I wouldn't be here. Without you I am not whole. This and everything else, I owe entirely to you. I love you.

About the Author

Erik McHatton's passion for horror literature began in grade school, and can be credited to an early fascination with the "Terrific Triples" horror collections of Helen Hoke. In those books, he plumbed the depraved depths of Poe, CAS, Dunsany, Bloch, Bradbury and more and was forever after put under the spell of those masters. He began writing fiction seriously in 2019, and has since been published several times in print and online publications such as *Cosmic Horror Monthly*, *Vastarien*, *Tales to Terrify*, and *Lovecraftiana*. His story, "The Man Who Collected Ligotti," was chosen to appear in the Ligotti tribute issue of *Cosmic Horror Monthly*, and was among the stories included in Tenebrous Press's *Brave New Weird, Vol. 3* which collected the best new weird horror of 2024. He currently lives in Kentucky with his beautiful wife and kids, along with dear friends and family; surrounded on all sides.

Reading Advisories

"Straw World"
    suicide, gore, abuse, animal death, gun violence

"Knocks"
    child death, starvation

"We Must Be Rabbits"
    emotional abuse, kidnapping, hostages, torture

"The Success of Dover's Glen: A Study in Four People"
    depression, suicide

"Station 42"
    gore, animal death, emotional abuse, misogyny, murder

"Timmy Thomerson's Turn"
    child death, bullying, gore

"The Face Dealer"
    torture, gore

"The Last Case of Dr. Jonah Wexley Abbott"
    murder, gore, abuse, mental health hospitalization, terminal
    illness

"On the Night Bus"
    anxiety, ageism, alcoholism

"Something's Off About Wizzle"
    assault

"Where We Are, Where We Were, and Where We Will Always Be"
    abortion, sexual abuse, animal death, bullying, cancer, child abuse,
    pedophilia

"In Carnality"
    none

"The Man Who Collected Ligotti"
    child abuse, anxiety, depression, kidnapping, stalking, torture

"Demodorum"
    gore, abuse, depression, death, torture